THE POTENTIAL HAZARDS OF HESTER DAY

Mercedes Helnwein

Simon & Schuster
New York · London · Toronto · Sydney

SIMON & SCHUSTER
1230 Avenue of the Americas
New York, NY 10020

First Simon & Schuster trade paperback edition February 2008

SIMON & SCHUSTER and colophon are registered trademarks of Simon & Schuster, Inc.

For information regarding special discounts for bulk purchases, please contact Simon & Schuster Special Sales at 1-800-456-6798 or business@simonandschuster.com.

Designed by Dana Sloan

Manufactured in the United States of America

10 9 8 7 6 5 4 3 2 1

Library of Congress Cataloging-in-Publication Data

Helnwein, Mercedes, 1979–
The potential hazards of Hester Day : a novel / Mercedes Helnwein.
   p. cm.
Summary: Dreading a future as dull as her dysfunctional family's, quirky eighteen-year-old Hester marries a near-stranger and sets out from Florida on a road trip with him and her ten-year-old cousin, Jethro, only to be derailed by a self-avowed "Jesus Freak" and a national news alert that she is a drug-abusing kidnapper.

ISBN 10: 1-4165-7466-2 (pbk. : alk. paper)
ISBN 13: 978-1-4165-7466-8
[1. Self-actualization (Psychology)—Fiction. 2. Social isolation—Fiction. 3. Family problems—Fiction. 4. Automobile travel—Fiction. 5. Runaways—Fiction. 6. Marriage—Fiction.] I. Title.

PZ7.H375955Pot 2008
[Fic]—dc22   2007027136

To my parents

THE
POTENTIAL
HAZARDS
OF HESTER DAY

INTRODUCTION

MY PARENTS named me Hester Louise Day. Hester after a dead sister, Louise after a dead aunt, and Day after some dead man way back when, who started this family somewhere in Europe on a dark, horny night.

Early childhood:

I have a hard time remembering it, to tell the truth. It must have been boring. All I can remember is pink wallpaper of bears holding umbrellas—and a thick blanket with matching ruffled pillows, also with some kind of pointless pattern to it.

Major social events:

When I was five, I won an award at school for a bean necklace I made.

When I was nine, I lost my good reputation forever. That is, I broke a kid's nose in school—I don't remember why really, except that it had something to do with an eraser. But after that, I was never again looked at in quite the same way.

When I was fifteen, a boy outside the public library looked at my legs and raised his eyebrows at me when I looked back. I spent that night wondering about how to take a compliment.

Friends:

I had one of those growing up—a little kid who always wore cowboy hats and liked to wrestle furniture. His name was Mark and he lived somewhere on our street and was going to be a cowboy when he grew up, but I happened to know for a fact that his parents had already decided he was going to become a lawyer. I never told him.

We ended up sitting next to each other in the playground one fall day when we were four. We looked at each other with huge, blank eyes—and then he asked me for how much money I would eat a human toe. We became friends without further ado.

When we were thirteen, Mark moved away to Kansas City and left me alone with my family and my puberty. The loneliness was shattering, but I never realized how terrible it actually was until much later when I looked back at that period. I realized that I was only able to survive it *because* I was thirteen at the time.

Mental attributes:

I never suffered from interesting psychological problems, and when I *did*, I would always find out later that it was a false alarm—that my psyche had not been dented after all—and I was still as easy and unaffected as the day the doctor pulled me out of my mother.

I tried sometimes to be tackled by mysterious depressions and problems that would make life interesting. I tried to be engulfed in frowns that nobody could possibly understand and so be looked upon as a beautiful, tragic enigma. That was my ambition for a while—to be incomprehensible. I realized later that I had been incomprehensible most of the time anyway, just not in an advantageous, romantic way.

Physical attributes:

I was small for my age at seventeen, and I had a round face, which always left me looking at least three years younger. My wardrobe consisted mainly of clothes predating 1970. This had little to do with fads. I just couldn't stand the thought of my parents paying for my clothes—something about that made me feel nauseous. So when I needed new clothes I went to the only places my personal financial situation would allow me to go— thrift stores. I was particularly fond of strange repetitive patterns, stripes, and strong, solid colors.

My skin was white as chalk, and I had ruby lips that liked to smile at things. That smile, I guess, was the first barrier to wistful romanticism. I was too blunt in my solutions, too deranged in my ideals, too simple in my emotions.

I had grass-green eyes and brown hair that might have been black. Once every few months I got out the kitchen scissors and chopped it off somewhere between my chin and my shoulders, depending on the angle I happened to be holding the scissors at.

But the most characteristic quality I had was my cheeks always being the color of cherries. Sometimes I looked at myself in the mirror and realized I looked like a Technicolor cartoon. People usually thought I wore a distasteful amount of rouge, and for a while I rubbed ivory foundation over my cheeks before I went to school.

Health:

They always said my liver was weak, but I don't trust doctors. I'd just as soon listen to a fire hydrant on medical issues. Whatever someone in a lab coat and a stethoscope around his neck told me, I generally believed the opposite to be true.

I did start smoking at thirteen, though, mainly because life at the time called for a bad habit that was also illegal. Whenever I thought I had developed bronchitis, I'd give it up; but as soon as I realized it was a false alarm, I'd strike up another match.

Family:

My dad was an architect, and my mother was one of those women who ran around in inoffensive cream-colored suits and hats, going to barbecues and charity gatherings. Hannah, my older sister, was preparing to study psychology.

It was rumored in the neighborhood that we were a wonderful specimen of suburban life. Other families used to look over at us while sprinkling their lawns, and you could see in their eyes that they labeled us as healthy and intact. I never understood what gave them that impression, because you could have randomly pointed at any white-trash family and they would have been more civilized than we were.

Sometimes my mother got it into her head that she was proud of her youngest daughter and she'd take me along to weddings, funerals, family reunions, Easter egg hunts, or breast cancer fund-raisers. But by the end of the day, she would usually realize that she wasn't all that proud of me after all. With time, all such efforts were abandoned, leaving me to quietly lead the existence of a young mushroom in my room.

By the time I was fourteen I was completely unrelated to humanity. I wasn't particularly absentminded or ignorant—au contraire, I had studied many subjects extensively (so extensively, in fact, that you might wonder if some of the bizarre facts I had acquired would ever see the light of day again)—I had made thorough use of the public library and had developed a very intimate relationship with classic literature. But I was a Stone Age creature in modern society. I didn't know what to say or when to say it, how to greet, how to take my leave of a crowded dinner table, what to expect or when to expect it, when to laugh or when to frown disapprovingly. But it was more than just a matter of etiquette—I wasn't familiar with the human race and their emotions, their ideals, their concepts. I was so left alone by my species that I really didn't have a clue as to what they were all about. I didn't know what I was supposed to consider a good thing and what I should consider less good. My actions were blunt and often too fast. My solutions were momentous and extreme.

I didn't like my family all that much, just like they didn't like *me* all that much. I want to say that I hated my family, but that would be a lie. Fact is, I didn't truly hate anyone until I was about nineteen and had a conversation with the sales representative of a phone company.

Hometown:

Midsized towns in this country are all the same if you ask me. There is something depressing just in the way the breeze pushes trash around empty streets. Or the way people eat at the food courts in malls, with their shopping bags at their ankles. The way carpets smell in hyper-air-conditioned bank buildings. The way cops have nothing better to do than pull you over for crossing double-yellow lines.

Florida—the appendix of this great country. Every time you open a front door you're smothered by something or other: the humidity, the sun—maybe just last night or maybe the premonition of tomorrow. It's all stagnant. I think sometimes everything must have stood still at a very awkward point in history there. Not the "good old days," but rather some moldy moment in the eighties that left us with no heritage. After all, what are we associated with? Oranges, old ladies with purple hair, sunshine, and tourists.

Then there is the nature, which is beautiful if you like postcards. In the evenings the palm trees are burnt against pink skies, and the light reflects off the Gulf of Mexico, rippling all the way to the horizon. I used to tell myself that this was the roof of all those fish—the ceiling to some massive living room. One thing that never failed to comfort me about home was the nighttime breeze. No matter if you're standing outside the Laundromat waiting for oversized blankets to finish washing, or strolling down the beach, watching hippies play the drums—there's always something nice about the way the air licks your neck after the sun's gone down. And then comes the morning, and the sun fries you into the liquid asphalt.

But who knows, my descriptions of home could be completely lopsided. Maybe it's really paradise. "Hell" and "paradise" are two very interchangeable words. Let's leave it at that.

stood talking animatedly to a small audience of parents. They hugged and then she joined in the animated talk. The rest of us stood there for a few seconds, vehemently wishing we were not standing there.

"Good job, honey," my dad said after a while.

I said, "Thanks."

"We really didn't know sometimes if you'd ever get here," he added, looking at his watch. "I just want you to know how proud we are."

I said, "Cool."

We lapsed back into silence, and since there was nothing better to do, I slid off the ribbon from my diploma and rolled it open. It proved to be a marble-patterned paper, thick, covered in various signatures and writings—and imprinted into its strong eggshell color, I found the name "Ronald Peterson" spelled out neatly in cheap calligraphy. With a lopsided smile, I let it roll back together again.

I was glad they gave me the wrong diploma. It sort of made up for the fact that this graduation ranked second to a pornography awards ceremony. Everything about it was so sadly hollow. Everyone who walked over that stage brought along their own little custom-made tragedy. Their shiny robes tugging in the wind, dwarfing them; their silly hats bearing all that significance, turning their proud smiles into sad deformities. It made me feel sick with a sense of sympathy. Not the typical Salvation Army type of sympathy that makes you feel all warm and special, but the kind that sits heavy and dark in your stomach. The one that gives you a feeling like you're drowning in blackstrap molasses.

Maybe all my feelings were entirely unfounded and the fact that my stomach was crawling up my throat only had to do with my own shortcomings. Maybe I had strange phobias. Maybe I had a vitamin deficiency. Or maybe I was just born under the wrong star. Who knows? And who cares? It didn't change the fact that every time I looked around myself, I cringed. It didn't help the fact that they all looked like pale, undercooked sausages, without a hint of a shadow of a clue in the world. They would be deep-fried without ever knowing it. The unfortunate ones would lead painful lives, dejected or jealous, watching their dreams being lived by others. The lucky ones would live their dreams.

Maybe the worst of it all is that after eighteen years on this earth, their dreams amounted to shit. Everyone wanted to personify the life of a TV sitcom, to be as desirable as the people whose intense grins represent the many magazines that lie next to toilets, on coffee tables, and in the waiting rooms of dentist offices.

Life would pass them all by. Every one of them.

"See, now there's a nice smile," my aunt whispered, nodding at a graduate who happily posed for a picture, holding his diploma high in the air like some kind of tae kwon do trophy.

"Everyone knows that young man is going places. They can hang that picture up on the wall and be proud, because he looks happy—he doesn't look like a train just drove over his right foot."

She gave me a meaningful, dark look.

"Can't argue with you there, Aunt Emma."

Aunt Emma hated it when someone didn't want to argue with her.

We stood around a little longer, looking like a herd of uninspired cows, until eventually my mom returned and we all followed her to the car.

"Honestly, you could all learn how to mingle a little," she said, like it was starting to be a drag the way she had to be the backbone to this family of retards.

The prom hadn't been much better, by the way, except that I accidentally set off the fire alarm by smoking right underneath it. I hadn't intended to cause havoc—I hadn't even intended to be there at all, actually, but my mother insisted I go. For her, it was the most unthinkable thing in the universe that a girl would decline to put on a dress and watch all the undercooked sausages moving around the dance floor with mock sentimentality. I wasn't about to put myself through all that, and I did try to get out of it, but I really didn't stand a chance.

"Mom, I really don't want to go," I had told her as we drove home from the dry cleaner.

She looked at me with a dead-serious twitch of her lip. After a black silence she said, "Did nobody ask you to the prom?"

"It's not that," I said, locking my eyeballs firmly on the glove compartment to keep them from rolling. "I'd just rather not go."

"Don't worry. We'll get Larry from next door to go with you. You can't let on that anything is the matter when you get there. Prom is the first and probably the most crucial point in one's life. Larry is in college, so you'll probably even be one up against the others."

Oh Lord.

"Trust me when I say that success in life is based on your prom in more ways than you think," she added after a thoughtful pause.

"Maybe for some careers it would matter," I said, doubting what I had just said in a serious way, "but I don't think it would make a difference for me."

"It matters. It always matters."

"What if someone wanted to be a professional surfer?"

She looked at me sternly. "That's not funny."

"Okay, I'll go," I simply said. "But why do I have to go with Larry?"

"Because, if you show up at a prom alone, you are done for right there and then. You're better off just dying in a car wreck on the way there."

"Well, I'll just call George, if you don't mind," I said, a little bewildered. "He asked me to go with him a while back."

She looked over. Her eyes were large and bright and looked like they were illuminated from the inside. She couldn't have looked more ecstatic if she'd had a religious revelation.

"So you *were* asked!"

"Well, yeah, but I told them all I wasn't going."

"'Them *all*'? Plural? Oh, that's wonderful. You have no idea how wonderful that is!"

And that is how it came that I sat in George's car in a purple prom dress that evening. He was nervous, and I felt sorry for him. He tried to have a conversation and I fucked it up in various ways. I thought I was just breaking the ice, but I guess you've got to be careful where you lodge that ax.

"So what made you change your mind?" he asked as we pulled out of the driveway. "I thought you said you weren't interested in going to the prom."

"Well, it wasn't so much that I changed my mind on my own account. You see, my mom is apparently part of a strange cult that worships the 'wholesome American way,' and if I would have refused to go to the prom, they'd have excommunicated her."

He tried to laugh and said, "Yeah, I know what you mean." And I was considerably surprised that he knew what I meant.

We drove down a block in silence before he apologized for not having commented on my dress.

"I wouldn't have commented on my dress either if I were you," I said.

"No, but I *should* have said something."

"Why?"

"You just look really beautiful, and I should have said that earlier," he said very earnestly. "I want you to know that that was the first thing I noticed, but I forgot to mention it because your mom was saying all those things, and I was listening to her, and then I thought for a second that I locked my keys in the car, so I was just distracted. But anyway, I really meant to tell you as soon as you opened the door that you look—stunning. Just so you know."

I raised my eyebrows, feeling a little uneasy at the fact that he had said "stunning." It reminded me somehow of a little kid handling power tools.

"Well, thanks," I said.

"Thank you for changing your mind."

"Gee, you're flattering me into a bloody pulp here. I told you it has nothing to do with me. You should be thanking my mom for being a nut."

Short silence.

"Hester, I *mean* it." His voice came loaded with childish emotions.

"You mean *what*?"

"All this that I'm saying. I don't want you to get the wrong impression. I know it was rude not to mention your dress, and I'm not like that usually."

I played with the window button, letting the window slide up and down.

"You couldn't do anything wrong if the U.S. government paid you for it, George, so relax."

"I'm totally relaxed. I just want you to know that I'm not taking this lightly."

"I wish you would."

"Why?" he asked, diverting his eyes from the road to rest them on me.

"Well, because it's not like we're going to end up losing our virginity tonight under the starry sky, out on the football field."

"Of course not." His eyes went quickly back to the road.

I realized then that I had just driven a sledgehammer through everything that prom stood for. All that wonderful hope crushed—extinguished mercilessly before the auditorium halls had even been reached. I felt terrible.

The auditorium was decorated with terrible taste and sad attempts at creating a special significance for this night. The band was quite possibly worse than the decorations. A few of the girls bombarded me with vigorous hugs and high-pitched screams, which caught me off guard, because I didn't really know any of them that well. I mean, I knew some of their heads from the back, and some of them from the lunch line or as characters from bizarre rumors—but I didn't *know* them. We never actually found it necessary to acknowledge one another's presence in the classrooms. Now I was lying in their perfumed arms, and their elaborate hairdos were bouncing around my neck. It was all kind of like we were at a mountaineers reunion and I just ran into the members of my first expedition up Mount Everest.

They said things like: "I love your dress!"

And I said: "Oh—thanks. Thanks."

My mother had bought my dress—it was bright purple, shiny,

and long with a stream of some kind of see-through blue material hanging down one side. I had no particular sentiments about it one way or another. My shoes looked like they were borrowed from the set of a World War II barn dance scene. They were the only pair of shoes that I had with heels. I looked ridiculous, and I was well aware of it in a detached sort of way.

The events of the night went by slowly. Some girl called Kelly was crowned prom queen. Some guy reached for a cup on the table so that his wrist could brush against my ass while I stood beside him. Someone with a lime-colored tuxedo burped the American anthem. Someone else began to cry and exclaim that he loved us all. A guy sitting opposite us at the table was continually trying to get his date to remember "that one scene in that one movie," and the girl was trying to make him notice her bra, which she had carefully pulled forth slightly from underneath her dress.

George talked to me about studying economics and his views on how the stock market would do in the upcoming year. I nodded and suppressed yawns and said things like, "Yep." And "Hell, yeah."

Eventually the conversation turned to how annoying paper cups are because if you use them too much they break through at the bottom. It was the first conversation that evening I kind of got into, and just when I thought I could breathe easily, George abruptly landed an uncomfortable kiss on my mouth.

I tried to smile at him when he drew back but my lips were immovable.

"Let's dance," he said.

The last thing I wanted to do was shake a goddamn leg.

"George, I'd rather just sit here and talk more about paper cups."

"Come on!"

He was one of those annoying people who grab your hand when you don't wanna dance and use their whole weight to tear you off the chair. I never understood why these people exist. Seems like they make it their life's mission to find reluctant dancers and wrestle them onto dance floors. I wonder sometimes if they're a religious community.

I sighed, and before there was much to be done about it, we were moving back and forth as blandly as possible. The music was calm and someone sang about true love in a way that made it obvious he was getting paid minimum wage for it. I felt life closing in on me: here I was slow-dancing with a future economic analyst—next thing, I'd probably be getting him a beer out of the fridge after a long day of work at the office. Wasn't that how it went?

I broke off and stepped back.

"George, would you mind if I'm brutally honest with you right now?"

He looked scared. "No, go ahead."

"Well, how can I put this? I guess I'm just feeling a little—a little like my insides are being pulled out of me while I'm looking on and seeing every detail of it. Mind if we stop dancing?"

"Uh, no . . ."

"Sorry," I said as we stood awkwardly against the wall again with our magenta-colored drinks. "I wasn't trying to freak you out."

"That's okay," he said, but of course he had no idea what he'd just labeled as okay. George would never have a clue. He was sweet and sincere and good—and he'd be one of those men barbecuing on Sundays with a checkered apron, oblivious to wars and famine and government conspiracies. Quite possibly, he'd lead the happiest life of the whole goddamn graduating class. I wasn't about to get in his way.

"George," I began freshly, "will you please stop thinking all these sentimental things about me? I'm not that kind of girl. I don't want someone to flatter me on my dress—especially not when it looks like shit. What *I* think is 'okay' is so far removed from what *you* consider 'okay.' There are whole worlds between us."

George still didn't understand. His eyes blinked excessively and nervously. He took a sip from his drink and looked over, trying to decide on what to say. I sighed. I was running out of ideas for making sense to him.

"Look, there are not only worlds between you and me—there are worlds between me and everything *else* too. Maybe not just worlds—maybe whole universes. I don't think I'm naturally supposed to be here—I think something must have gone wrong. I think my parents conceived me by total accident."

"You shouldn't be so hard on yourself," he said.

"What are you talking about? I'm never hard on myself."

I could see I was intimidating George, so I put my hand on his shoulder and said, "You see that girl over there?"

I pointed to a girl sitting alone in a chair, kind of pretty except that her legs were skinny in the wrong places. Her brand-new shoes matched her sequined dress. There was glitter on her cheeks that you could see from a mile away, and her pink lipstick was perfectly applied onto unhappy lips that knew they were all made up for probably no reason.

"Yeah," said George.

"Well, you should go over there and ask her to dance."

He looked at me, a little distraught.

"Hester, I can't just—just stop feeling things for one person and start feeling things for someone else just like that."

"How do you know? Try it," I said.

"Look, Hester—"

"I'm not making small talk here—I'm dead serious. Will you please just trust me on this one?"

I watched him walk uneasily toward her, and probably the only reason he went over there at all was because he was scared to death of what I might do otherwise. She looked up at him, they exchanged a few words, and after looking around, a little surprised, the girl stood up and they walked off. I watched them move around the dance floor. I could see George exchanging his routine dialogue with her and I could see the girl giggling and reacting to it as though they had practiced it all earlier. There was so much relief reflected on him after what I had just put him through that his confidence soared up high—evolution seemed to speed up miraculously and from an amoeba grew a man.

I crawled into a dark corner, where I lit a cigarette and put it into my mouth. I coughed and stared lifelessly out at the auditorium—blaring with music, obscured by dark figures and balloons.

Somewhere after my sixth cigarette the fire alarm went off.

GIVE YOU THE DEVIL
IF YOU ACT KINDA HARD

NOBODY WITH the name of Day had done anything conspicuous for quite a while. During Prohibition we didn't drink moonshine, and during the gold rush we didn't rush for gold. We just didn't do those things. A long time ago we came from Europe, and I like to believe that we were different over there—that we led weird existences, had bizarre ideals, and strove for abnormal goals. On American soil, we've always been the kind of people who were regarded with solemn respect. Respect so rigorous that it threatened to pull a tendon. We have always been upright, our intentions have always been severely good, and our houses were always covered in immaculate paint jobs. Our decency was supreme. Only on closer examination would it have been discovered that there was nothing to respect.

I never meant to be particularly different. But I was born legally into the family on a dull October day, and right from my birth my parents knew I was the one who had the genes that hadn't seen light since the days of Europe.

Once I was done with school, I intended to do nothing normal anymore. Happiness seemed something like the devil's cupcake recipe. It seemed to be a trap—a drug like heroin. I felt true happiness would have a different name, and you couldn't come by it the way everyone thought. I wanted nothing more than to see something that would leave me unsettled—or settled, depending on how you want to look at it. Something that would be real—as real as those old records, where the songs live through a troubled voice, accompanied by the crackling of a guitar or a battered piano. Songs recorded long ago, in hotel rooms with strange-patterned wallpaper, and archaic city life crawling beyond the window. Way back. Blood, sweat, and tears were real, and nobody went to see a shrink. Back when people knew how to put things into sentences . . . *"that new way of lovin', swear to God it must be best. All those Georgia women won't let Willie McTell rest."*

I sat on my bed. Above me on a lonesome nail hung my diploma, framed in a fake gold frame with the name "Ronald Peterson" proudly displayed. My mother found this to be the most distasteful idea of a joke ever. *I* found it comforting. It made me laugh. It was the perfect souvenir of my years in school.

"Hester, why are you making everything so difficult?"

"I don't know."

"What's the matter with you?"

"I don't know."

My eyes were heavily set on the bottom right-hand corner of my room, where the door met the carpet. My mother and father stood in front of me. I was just in the process of refusing to go to college, and my mother regarded me with bloodshot, nervous eyes like in cartoons.

"I thought I was making things easier," I said.

"Easier my *ass*."

I stared at her blankly with no comeback in sight.

"Look, Hester, the fact of the matter is that you have no clue what you're talking about—you never did. You might *mean* well, but in this case you really have to listen to your father and me. This is just too important—this is your life."

Suddenly, I knew *exactly* what to say. I knew how to phrase it, how to lay it out, how to make a point that would shatter everything in sight—I knew how to present my case on red velvet. It was one of those random moments of brilliance.

"Mom, the thing is—"

"There is no '*thing*,' Hester. I've already told you the only 'thing' there is!"

The sentence squirmed in my head like a dissected worm. Ruined. I didn't remember the point I was going to make.

"College is important."

"Relatively," I offered up.

"No, it's not!" she said, emphatically squeezing the leg of a stuffed elephant that was lying on my bed. "It's not relative. It's college—it's what one does at your age—there's nothing relative about it."

"It's more relative than most things," I carefully contradicted her. "College is a place where a bunch of kids go because they'd be torn to shreds if they dared to set foot in the real world. Kids go to college so they get to play high school all over again—only they probably learn even less and do more drugs. They get another colorful piece of paper to frame and hang on their walls, and

later, when they're old they get to talk about 'the good old days.'
I'm just not interested in all that."

My mother's brow became troubled, and she didn't even *pretend* to understand half of what I'd just said. Whenever I tried to make a point, I was well aware that to my mother everything came out sounding like a malfunctioning robot spurting out beeping noises.

"Look, whatever you're trying to—to *tell* me here, it's all beside the point," she said. "I'm not going to let you ruin your whole life, just because you have some hippie ideas about college."

"I don't have hippie ideas."

"Hester, honestly, this is *not* funny. I'm very serious. There is no way that you will get around going to college. And even if it's painful for a while, you will thank us later on when you have life properly set up."

"You want me to pack my bags and go to a place where for thousands of dollars I get to waste four more years of my life?"

"How can you talk like that—like you ever paid for anything yourself? You don't even know what real money *is!*"

"Maybe. But if it's not my money, that's all the more reason not to throw it out the nearest window."

It looked like she was close to tears. She was always on edge. My father, on the other hand, was always as far removed from the edge as you could possibly be.

"Mom, what did *you* get out of college?"

She thought a while. My mother was as ignorant as a doorknob, so I was particularly interested in what she'd come up with for this one.

"I met your *father* in college," she said.

I burst into a hard smile that I couldn't suppress.

"Don't roll your eyes at me," my mother said.

Actually, I hadn't rolled my eyes. I knew better. It had been four years since I last rolled my eyes at my parents. My amusement, however, was something that came and went entirely of its own accord. As long as I can remember, people were always telling me that something was not funny. I've always laughed at the supposed wrong times and places, but to me "wrong times" didn't exist.

"Listen, Hester, if I hadn't gone to college you wouldn't have any eyes to roll right now. Think of it that way."

"That's brilliant, Mom," I said. "That sounds like one of those offbeat religious flyers that people hand out in front of enemy churches!"

My mother ripped the alarm clock from its socket and threw it out the window. I looked after her with a lost face as she tore out of the room. Discussions often ended like this. I blurted out something stupid, my mom threw an object out the window, and my dad silently sprouted roots in the carpet, probably thinking of his secretary bending over to pick up a pencil she'd dropped. I had long ago lost any interest in feeling the guilt that I was supposed to feel, and I looked at it all as if it were happening in some house across the country.

"Well, I'll see you at dinner," my dad said, still standing by my closet door, still looking out the window with his protein shake and an expression almost as blank as mine.

I knew that this meant I was going to college. My father never actually had to say what he meant to make a point come across like a Supreme Court verdict. I crossed my arms and watched silently as he strolled out of the room.

Is that really how easy it was? Is that all it took to map out the remainder of my life—a protein shake? And me just sitting there under the diploma, wondering whether my dad really thought those little pastel-colored drinks would give him the six-pack the man on the box had? Is this how futures are created?

I suddenly began to feel overwhelmingly moldy, and for a short moment I entertained the thought that maybe I could do something about it. But what? *How?* I shifted my position on the bed as though that would change anything, but nothing came to mind. Maybe it would be easier to give up the effort wasted on propping your legs with all your stubborn might against fate. Could it be possible that it was easier just to be satisfied? Who was I to think that I could avoid the blueprint anyway? Why were these preschool dreams still clinging to me? Kids usually gave up wanting to be astronauts and cowboys and queens and pirates by the time they slapped their high school books down on their desks. And me? I was still every bit a five-year-old.

I knocked my lamp down with a feverish movement of my elbow and watched as the lampshade ripped from its wire structure.

Sitting in the passenger side of the car later that day, my eyes accidentally caught sight of a billboard with two wide-eyed children, looking wistfully out at me from above the catchy phrase "All they want for Christmas is a family." I thought it was odd that orphans were already writing their Christmas wish list when it was only the beginning of July. The light turned green, the car began to move again, and I turned my head away.

I looked at my mother's glazed face. The sunlight had begun to melt her thick makeup. Her face betrayed that everything was dead and buried in her stupid life, and she seemed only too happy about it.

Then I thought, why not adopt one of those kids whose lives were advertised on billboards?

The idea was just absurd enough for me to really get my hooks into it hard. The more I thought about it the less sense it made; and the more it thrilled me. I lay in bed all that night with my eyes open and visions appearing on the ceiling. I saw exactly how peculiar my life could possibly be—if only I decided to wink and go with my instincts when my smiles turn crooked. Those smiles that people smile when they eat sour candy or unripe cherries, twisting their mouths from the distaste but, all the same, with sugar on their lips. Those smiles are always worth their weight in gold. At least in my case they are. When I smiled like that and my cheeks flushed, I knew my ideas were impossible—and, sadly, they'd be the most delicious ones. I never could do much with my delicious thoughts. I could play with them, but I couldn't realize anything. I never could. I never would.

I turned over and watched the shadow of a palm tree against my closet door. How do you realize wishes like wanting to adopt a kid? My purpose on this earth had never been to erect barricades in front of my parents and heroically wave tattered red flags in the wind. But then it occurred to me: if I just this *once* grabbed good hold of these lunatic ideas, then maybe I'd be a little less to blame for my own mediocre misery.

Shit. I had a point.

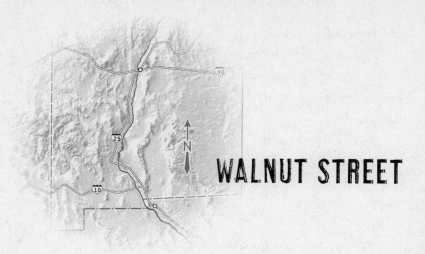

WALNUT STREET

THE ORPHANAGE closest to us sat on the outskirts of town. It was an old-fashioned brick building, painted yellow, with a courtyard and high fences around it to keep the basketballs from rolling into the street. It looked neat and hygienic. I was somewhat disappointed, to tell you the truth—I had read *Oliver Twist* enough times to know what an orphanage ought to look like, and this was pitiable. I might as well be going to a bank to start a savings account. Everything here seemed so straight and polished in some way—it sort of made me wish my parents had dropped me off here when I was born.

"I'd like to adopt a kid—*child*. I'd like to adopt a child."

I sat in the office on a green leather chair that was really made out of plastic, wishing I hadn't said "kid." A fat woman sat behind the desk, staring at me intensely while she played with a stapler. Her size and the flower design on her dress made her look clumsy; but the way her eyes zeroed in on me made me want to duck for cover. She made me nervous in a dozen ways—especially now that I had sounded so cheap. I already felt like I had committed a felony.

"How old are you?"

"Eighteen—in October."

She kept all feelings and emotions securely hidden. She didn't even raise her eyebrows when it would have been the proper thing to do.

"So you're seventeen?"

"Technically. Until October, yes."

"October isn't until a few months—you're aware of that, aren't you?"

"Sure."

"Well, the legal age for adoption is eighteen here."

"I know."

We shared a mutual stare of uncertainty.

"What made you decide to adopt?" she asked eventually, with a sudden deep and fascinated frown.

"I've always felt the desire to take someone into my home and give them the family life that they were deprived of. I think every child has the right to have his own home—his own backyard and his own tire swing. Every child has the right to have parents at her side, wearing party hats on her birthday. Every child has the right to hear the sports channel from the next room and know that his father is watching basketball. Or to hear the sizzling of a pan, knowing that her mother is making her favorite meal. This is how I grew up. This intimacy of parental love made me who I am. And I just think no one has the right to grow up without it. It hurts me to think that so many children never know this sense of security—this tailor-made love."

I had found that speech in a little adoption pamphlet that happened to be lying around the library the day before. Some lady who had adopted a child from Romania had summed up her experiences in those words. It took me all morning to get it down cold, but I managed. For the longest time I couldn't quite decide if it was too sentimentally loaded or whether I was just a cold human being—I decided on the latter eventually and calculated that it would be just the sort of thing to hit home with normal people.

"Well," she said, "that's a lovely way of putting it."

And after a pause, she added: "But for all I know, you could have memorized that from somewhere."

"Sure," I said. "I could have memorized that from somewhere. Technically I could have memorized everything I say off of somewhere. And so could you."

She wasn't too impressed. "Are you married?"

"Yes."

My heartbeat started picking up its pace and I became warm in the face. It seemed that this interview was going to fry me alive, and I didn't have the sense to play it safe.

"Being married is an advantage in most cases," she said, pulling out a brochure from a desk drawer. "These children are all very emotionally vulnerable, you see. We don't want to subject them to instability."

"Oh, I know."

I was nervous now, and all I could look at and think about was her large waist and her plump little body as it moved around the room. Her thick legs, the padding on the sides of her ass, and the milky-blue vein embedded in the fat of her arm.

"I have to be honest with you," she said. "Although it might be legal to adopt at eighteen, I would never consider letting someone that young adopt a child. Quite frankly, I wouldn't dream of it. How can I trust someone at that age with the life of a child?

We're not talking about a hamster here—we are talking about a living, breathing human being."

I said nothing, because I found her point to be a valid one. My sister, for example, was nineteen at the time and I certainly would not have trusted her with the life of a hamster.

The lady sighed, slightly bored, looking out her office window, which overlooked the playground. "And you're not eighteen yet anyway."

"I know, but I was hoping time would take care of that."

Slapping down the brochure in front of me, she said, "I suggest you read through this, and come back when you're of legal age to adopt."

"Thank you," I said, weakly reaching out to take hold of the papers.

I walked back through the halls, trying to notice the children's drawings lining each side. I've always wanted children's drawings all over my walls, and I began to wonder whether the kid I'd adopt would draw a lot.

My state of mind was relatively calm, considering that I'd have to get married now. The palms of my hands were moist from the fat lady's interview, and I felt slightly nauseated at the routines and procedures that were supposed to get you a kid. But getting married seemed only a mechanical duty that had to be performed in order to attain what promised to unravel my life, and that's really what I wanted—everything to be unraveled.

I had no more money left for a cab, and so I wandered through the streets with the adoption brochure in my hands until I found a bus. I took about three wrong buses in all, but eventually I took enough right buses to make it home by twelve thirty that night—

just in time to see my sister and a young man I'd never seen before doing very intimate things on our front porch.

"Hey," I said, walking by.

"Hester!" my sister shrieked. "For Christ's sake!"

"Sorry, Hannah," I said, fishing out my keys, "but I thought I'd use the front porch this evening to get into the house, rather than the drain pipe."

They disentangled themselves, and I realized that I did actually know the young man—he worked at the video store on the other side of town.

"Hey, Louis," I said.

"Hey, how are you, Hester?"

"Good. I thought you guys were just friends."

"Hester, will you get the hell out of here?" Hannah said.

"Yeah, sure," I said, pulling open the door.

"And if Hank finds out about this I'll have you submitted to a mental institution once I'm a psychologist," she added.

Hank was her boyfriend.

"I'll try to refrain from mentioning it in one of my many deep conversations that I have regularly with Hank," I said, rolling my eyes. I really marveled at her superior stupidity sometimes.

"And by the way, you wouldn't be able to commit anyone to a mental institution as a psychologist—you'd have to be a psychiatrist," I added.

"Whatever! I'll have lots of psychiatrists as friends."

As soon as I had made it into my room and spread out on my bed, the door swung open. My mother stood in the doorway looking distraught, with the light from the hallway giving her a halo.

"Where on earth have you been, Hester?" she said quietly and intensely. "I was worried sick!"

Once every three months or so my mother found it necessary to be freaked out about me coming home late. This was apparently one of those nights. It wasn't even so much that she actually wanted to know where I'd been—it was more the thrill of living in something akin to a Mexican soap opera. It was something she had to do when there wasn't enough drama in the rest of her life to keep her going.

"I got lost," I said.

"You had sex, didn't you?"

"No, not really—I got lost."

She tore into the room, straight to my window, and looked out of it dramatically.

"Hester, I thought we agreed we'd talk about that before you actually did it!"

Here we go.

"What is wrong with you these days?" she went on. "You're hardly ever at home—out until all hours of the night, and now this!"

"Mom, I just got on a few wrong buses."

She turned around.

"He didn't offer you drugs, did he?"

"No."

"Hester, you better stay away from drugs. You have an addictive personality, and you'd go from marijuana to heroin in no time. Are you listening at all?"

"Yeah, yeah, I'm listening. I'll stay away from weed. Don't worry about it."

"I'm serious."

"So am I."

There was a slight smile on her face. It always seemed like the days of her youth poured back into her head whenever she mentioned drugs.

"Let's not tell your father about this," she said from the doorway.

I agreed.

THE WAY THE COOKIE CRUMBLES

THE LIBRARY stood sorrowfully in the heat of midday like a lost cause. The only people who ever made use of it seemed to be a couple of senior citizens, and the whole population of bums in the town who surfed the Internet there each day or lounged around reading magazines. Sometimes there'd be some student researching the Boston Tea Party or some such annoying event in American history.

Inside, the temperature was almost below freezing. There were bad patterns on the carpet and a few tables and chairs that looked like they had been borrowed from a prison. And then there were rows of metal shelves that went from the floor to the ceiling and stretched out until they hit a wall. That was the fiction department.

The nonfiction department on the second floor was where the computers, the biography section, poetry, records, and magazines were. All the people that went to the second floor were either extremely serious about very deep things, or they were from the other end of the scale, abusing the library, checking their e-mails, and reading magazines. I often wondered what group I belonged to, but I could never figure it out. When I went over to the shelves that stored valuable information, I usually looked up things so bizarre and detailed that it never seemed to qualify as serious. And when I slunk over to suck on colorful magazines, I never took them seriously enough to qualify as intensely shallow. I guess depth is relative.

I pressed the elevator button and stood back. Beside me stood Philosophy Man. That's what I had begun calling him. He always spent hours on the second floor trying to find ties between philosophical theories and the art of poetry—or something like that. I had asked him once but was lost by the time he got to the third sentence.

"I already pressed the button," he said, indicating the elevator button.

"Cool."

"I'm just saying, I don't think it needs to be pressed twice."

"Well, I didn't know."

"Actually, seeing me standing here, waiting for the elevator, should have made it obvious that I had already pressed the button. It's not like anyone would stand in front of an elevator for fun."

He was always like that. He could have been only a few years older than me, but he liked to act like there was a thirty-year age difference between us. His clothes were always dark and looked like they would be much more practical in an expedition to the North Pole than in the suffocating summer. He never wore anything short-sleeved, and I was positive he would rather face a firing squad than touch a pair of shorts. He wore old-fashioned shoes and liked wearing things on his head that covered his straw-blond hair. His face was probably as pale as mine, but unlike my cheeks, which were orange, his face was evenly white. He had dark shadows under his eyes—he looked *off*, like something in a pantry that's past its "best by" date.

His comments were always razor-sharp and extremely unnecessary, but I didn't mind them because I happened to be amused by them. Mostly, I found him great to play with. He hated to be played with, which made playing with him all the more worth it. Maybe I really was as immature as he saw me.

The elevator still hadn't come. I began pressing the button over and over again.

"I don't think that's going to speed it up," he said stiffly.

"So?"

"So why are you doing that?"

" 'Cause I am," I said, smiling.

"Well, it's pointless."

"I know, but it's a free country."

"Are you fucking serious right now?"

"Yes."

Just then the elevator opened.

"Ah!" I exclaimed, walking in, "See, it worked."

He followed me. "It was already on its way."

He didn't say anything else. When the elevator doors opened again, he headed straight for the literary essays, and I made a sharp turn to the right for the computers.

"Did you make a reservation?" the lady behind the counter asked me.

"No," I said, "I didn't have time. This was a spur-of-the-moment thing. It's an emergency actually."

"Well, I'm sure it is," she said, "but I really can't let you use a computer just now because I already have people signed up for it on my list here. The next opportunity would be in an hour. Would you like to put your name down?"

"I know you don't believe me, but the problem is I'm dead serious," I said. "I have some research to do. I got myself into kind of a situation the other day, you see."

"Honey, please—won't you just put your name down and use a computer when it's your turn?"

I stepped back from the counter.

"No, I'm afraid in an hour everything might very well be too late. But thanks anyway. Oh, and I really didn't mean to say 'shit' before, by the way. It just slipped out."

I slunk off and grabbed a book about North American wildlife. Somewhere in the back of my head it occurred to me I hadn't even *said* "shit." Oh well. I figured one could never be too careful in this town. I took the wildlife book with me into the back of the library and sat down stubbornly between two high walls of shelves. The book was lying open on my lap. I stared at a picture of a groundhog for a while without reading anything. I never really figured out what made me bring books back into these remote areas of the library and just sit. Probably something corny, like the company of books gives me peace of mind. I was about to get intensely annoyed at myself for having such banal habits when I happened to look up to find Philosophy Man's blank stare tilted down at me.

"Howdy," I said apathetically.

He rolled his eyes almost as apathetically as I had said howdy.

"What are you doing here?" he asked.

"Me? What are *you* doing here? I thought you were into literature 'n shit."

"I am."

"This is the medical section."

"So?"

"You don't have some kind of disease, do you?"

"I'm a hypochondriac. I don't *have* diseases, I just fantasize about them."

"Oh."

"Plus I like looking at human anatomy books—it helps me with my poetry."

"Ah." I nodded thoughtfully. "Yeah, you look like you'd write poetry."

"Well, please forgive me for being a cliché," he muttered.

"Oh, I don't have a problem with it."

We proceeded to ignore each other for a short while.

"Excuse me, I need to get to those books," he said with a sudden cough.

I moved out of his way and watched him trail his fingers eagerly over the titles. In my head I was already beginning to wonder whether I'd have to change his name to Medical Man now.

"Hypochondriac, eh? What diseases are you most scared of?"

He seemed annoyed at my attempts to pass time pleasantly, but all the same, he knew too well what he was scared of most:

"Lung cancer."

After a short pause he added, "And heart attacks, I guess, but just because they're so unpredictable most of the time. Sometimes I get uneasy about Candida too, but that's rare. Mainly it's lung cancer."

"Paranoia of lung cancer is one thing I can't afford to have."

"You smoke?"

"Like a chimney." (I didn't really smoke like a chimney—but

it felt like it had to come out of my mouth just to make the conversation flow properly.)

"Well, in that case don't breathe on me," he said.

I breathed on him without further ado.

"Don't!"

I laughed and then stopped short and stared at him with large eyes. "You think me breathing on your knee is going to endanger your health?"

"I think you breathing anywhere ten miles within my vicinity will endanger my health."

I stood up. "Well, I'll go breathe somewhere else. See ya around, Philosophy Man."

That night, as I waited for my sister to come out of the bathroom, it occurred to me that God was perhaps trying to hint something to me. Not that I was certain there was a God, but in any case I felt like it would be good to look at this from a religious standpoint. Something about that deep, old southern trust in the Lord with enough superstition to make it interesting seemed very inviting. Instantaneously, I began to feel that childish warmth that spreads throughout your stomach when magic is at work.

Finally the door opened and, surrounded by steam and fake-apple perfumes, my sister strode out with a towel on her head.

"Hey, I just had a revelation!" I told her.

"*What?*"

She sounded offended.

"I just got a sign from above," I said. "God gave me a sign. I had divine contact."

She blinked as though I was shining a flashlight into her eyes. "Hester, *God!* You're fucking insane, did that ever occur to you?"

"Well—"

"And you *know* I hate it when you wait in front of the bathroom like that. It fucks up the timelessness factor of showering."

"What's the 'timelessness factor'?"

"Oh, forget it, okay? Just forget it."

Well, whatever. As far as I was concerned I had just given birth to a brilliant idea and was able to enjoy it twice as much because I was pretending to be a religious fanatic. This wasn't only an idea—it was now a holy revelation.

The next day I was back at the library.

"Hey!" I called, spotting Philosophy Man taking notes on one of the tables furthest removed from humanity.

He looked up and, seeing that it was me, quickly focused back on his notes.

"What're you doing?" I asked, sitting down next to him.

"Studying."

"Right on."

I watched him scribble things down. I watched the words being formed on his pad of paper with no interest in reading them.

He stopped. "Did you want something in particular?"

"Yeah, I did actually."

I thought a while. "Do you want me just to *tell* you or should we have some preliminary small talk?"

He sighed and stared at me from the end of his wits. "Skip the preliminary small talk."

"Okay." I leaned myself against the table. "Well, I thought we should maybe get married. I turn eighteen in October, so we can do it right after the seventh. What do you think?"

He stared long and hard. His eyebrows dropped over his eyes and then they went up again and his right eyelid began to quiver.

"Excuse me?" he asked at long last.

"I said, I think we should get married."

"Why?"

I shrugged my shoulders. "Why not? Is there really one good, solid reason why we *shouldn't* get married?"

"There are countless good, solid reasons."

"Like what?"

"What if I kill you?"

I waved his concern off. "What if a wild bull escapes from a zoo and kills us both? What if I choke on an olive pit and then accidentally cough it out, and it comes flying out so forcefully that it permanently damages your eye? Look, it's best to forget all about the what-ifs—they'll only make you go crazy."

He said nothing, but looked a little disturbed.

"Who ever heard of a flawless marriage anyway?" I went on. "It doesn't exist. We don't have to change a universal law. We'll just get by like they all do."

For a moment his eyes wandered over the papers scattered across his books, and then they fixed themselves back on my face. He looked lost.

"Is this your childish idea of love at first sight?"

"Fuck love at first sight! We both know that's just a myth. What I'm saying is that everything about our marriage would be so simple—there wouldn't be anything to it. Literally."

"I thought marriage was something deep and religious."

"I'm religious for all the wrong reasons, and I doubt I'm deep."

He rolled his eyes and began taking notes again.

"Well?" I asked, leaning into his face.

"Well, what?"

"Do you want to marry me?"

"No. Of course not. Now leave me alone."

I fixed my eyes on his. "Sure?"

"Please just do me a favor and don't come to the library for a whole day—just give me one day of peace!"

I stared at him a few seconds longer and then stood up.

I won't lie. I was a little depressed. I tried to figure out why someone would refuse to marry me. Sure, there were plenty of reasons that I could think of—and they were all solid as oak, but that's not what interested me. I wanted to know what reasons a different person would have for rejecting me so definitely and finally.

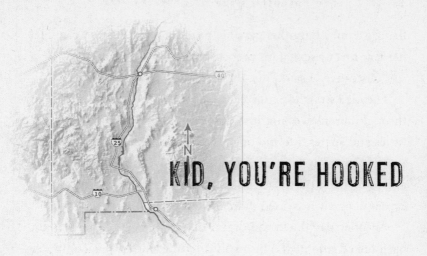

KID, YOU'RE HOOKED

IT WAS a Wednesday when I next walked through the old electric doors to the library. I had fulfilled Philosophy Man's wish and stayed away all of Tuesday. I wanted to stay away an extra day just to be good, and I very nearly made it too, but when the afternoon came to a burning peak, the tar on the streets seemed heavy and hot, my hands were lying restlessly in my lap with nothing to do, and I imagined I could hear the ticking of the clock downstairs intermingled with my mother's television. I had no choice but to jump up and run downstairs.

"Where are you going?" my mother called.

I told her I was going to the library.

"Oh, the 'library,'" she said sarcastically.

She liked to believe that my visits to the library were in fact outrageous visits to some member of the opposite sex's house—most likely someone who was the drummer of a terrible band that sold drugs out of their garage. I once told her that I couldn't possibly lose my virginity quite *that* often, but after I realized that being a troubled mother gave her peace of mind, I gave up and let her fear for my sexual innocence as much as she liked.

"Of course," I said, "just the 'library.'"

I headed straight to the record section at the library and leafed through about two hundred corny Christmas albums from the fifties and sixties. I found one album that I'd probably borrow if I didn't have any fines on my library card. I looked at it a while and put it back, partly because I *did* have considerable fees on my card and partly because I didn't own a record player anyway.

Another day down the drain. If I had come earlier I might have talked one of the bums into letting me use his computer time. The only thing that consoled me now was the fact that I stayed out of Philosophy Man's way—somehow that made me feel like a saint. He wanted so badly to have me out of his miserable existence that actually staying away from him made me feel pretty goddamn noble. And yet, the idea of getting married to Philosophy Man had been, sadly, ideal. It hurt somewhat to have to put it out of my head. How would I find a husband before my eighteenth birthday?

I got to my feet. My knees were red and hurt from kneeling on the carpet for all that time. I made my way toward the stairs just to make sure I wouldn't encounter him in the elevator. Funny thing was that as soon as I pulled open the door to the staircase, I stood face-to-face with Philosophy Man's gape.

We both stepped back in a mixture of guilt and surprise.

"Why are you taking the stairs?" I asked him.

"Why are *you* taking the stairs?"

"Because I was sure I wouldn't come face-to-face with *you*."

"I don't *always* use the elevator, you know."

"Well," I said defensively, "I tried my best. I stayed away all

yesterday, and today I came in late and stayed in the record section—I know you never go there—so I did my part. It's not my
fault you took the stairs."

He looked at me, and it was obvious that half of what I had
just triumphantly spat out didn't reach him.

"What do you mean?" he said. "I like going into the record
section every now and then. What makes you think I wouldn't go
there? I listen to records all the time."

There was another silence.

"That's beside the point," I said.

"What's the point, then?"

"The point is—the point is that it's okay if you don't want to
marry me. I have no beef—I'm not going to take a picture of you
secretly and have it printed on a T-shirt or anything. I don't even
like you. I just thought it would be neat to get married, that's all."

He frowned in concentration. It was hard talking to him
sometimes just because of the goddamn way he concentrated so
hard on something you had just finished saying. It made you feel
like you should be embarrassed about some aspect of yourself
without knowing what.

"People don't get married just because it would be 'neat,'" he
said.

For some reason I felt a swell of pity for him, but I guess more
than that I felt like giving him a flawless uppercut—preferably in
slow motion.

"Listen, I better go," I said. "I just had a cigarette a short while
ago, and I'm sure I'm breathing out traces of nicotine at you right
now."

He said nothing and I brushed past him. Once I got outside and
the library doors had shut automatically behind me, I squinted

critically at the horizon. I was wondering whether to go home and figure out how to get myself a husband, or strike up small talk with one of the bums lying on the grass. The library was surrounded by the park, so there was never a shortage of bums sunning themselves.

I decided to say hello to F. F was a bum whom I had known for quite a while. He used to work security at the White House but couldn't handle certain pressures, so he ended up here in the park with a small portable TV set that played everything in green. He now called himself F in order to slip more thoroughly into obscurity. He was a conspiracy theorist and always made for great conversations on humid, desperate afternoons.

"Hello, F!"

"Why, hello, little one," he said, turning over on the blanket he had thrown out under one of the palm trees.

"What's new?"

"Well," he said in a slow drawl, "nothing is ever new. Things are always the same. We're all goin' down. Slow but sure."

He was the most cheerful pessimist that ever existed. He gave his presentiments of doom with an innocent smile.

"Yep," I said, "you're right about that one."

"The only way to live these days is to take life on a small scale. Lie under a tree and let yourself worry about how to get your next burger. Those problems will keep you healthy in the head. They're healthier than wondering whether someone somewhere will push a red button and send all of God's creatures sky high."

He grinned at me, displaying a few missing teeth between the yellow ones still rooted into his gums. If ever there was an eerie way to send you down the chute into the darker side of the twilight zone, this man had the technique down.

"Well, here's money for your next burger," I said, handing him a few dollars. "At least I can solve *that* problem for you."

"You know, you're the one decent person in this whole town." I waved his compliments to hell.

"Maybe someday we'll be able to solve the other problem— the atomic mushroom one," I said.

While pushing the money I had given him into his shoe, he looked up suddenly, sharp and alert. "Well, you know what they say about—"

But before he could get any further than that, someone broke him off with a loud, egotistical "Hey!" The kind of voice the farmer uses to get the pigs back in their shed.

I turned around and found Philosophy Man standing about three feet behind me, hands in his pockets, books under his arm, and a black beanie pulled over his hair.

"Well, well. Haven't seen you in a while," I said.

He never took much notice of my comments and always went straight to what he had to say. "You were *serious* a few days ago when you said we should marry, right?"

"Of course. You think I go around proposing for the hell of it?"

"Because, listen," he went on, "I'm working on a new poem. It's kind of an epic poem actually—it'll be the length of an average novel, but all of it will be in verse. Anyway, the working title for it at the moment is 'Transplant,' and it tells the story of a turbulent marriage between the narrator and a woman who is a little slow—mentally. She is not really retarded in the medical sense, but she has a mind of a ten-year-old, so she's 'behind,' I guess you could call it."

I nodded my head. F stared at us and seemed to find our

conversation intriguing enough to ignore his quietly blaring TV screen.

Philosophy Man continued. "I like to work from experience. I feel if you really go through shit yourself, you're more likely to put it down on paper with the right kind of authority. I mean, I want to be able to *know* how to talk about frustration. It needs to be real. When people read 'Transplant' I want them to cringe. And I thought your proposal would come in handy here."

I believe I was speechless for a short moment in time. Words didn't seem to materialize in my head, and even less in my mouth. I simply stood and stared.

"Well," said F, as though to answer for me, "I'll be a monkey's uncle."

I guess that was more or less what I was thinking anyway.

"What do you say?" Philosophy Man asked, looking at me with his clean, blue eyes burning into my face. "Are you interested?"

I shrugged my shoulders. "Yeah, sure. If you want. Do you think I'll be good enough to play the part of the retarded wife with issues, though?"

He beamed sincerely into my face. "Don't worry about it. You'll be great."

I wasn't very sure to what extent this was a compliment, but it was the first time he smiled and it felt too cozy for me to worry about the intent of it.

"All right. I guess we're engaged then, huh?"

"Yeah, I guess," he said. "Listen, I have to go right now. You said October seventh?"

"Yeah, that's my birthday."

"Okay, October seventh."

He turned and began to make his way to the parking lot while

I stared after him. Before he had gotten very far he turned around and fixed his eyes on me once more.

"Hey, what's your name, by the way?"

"Hester."

"What's your last name?"

"Day."

He thought a while, no doubt computing how well this name would blend into the brilliance of his epic poem. After a few seconds of an absentminded stare, his face came back to life.

"I'm Fenton Flaherty."

And with that he disappeared around the corner. It was the end of Philosophy Man. The beginning of Fenton. I remained dazed in the bizarre significance of these last few moments.

"Well! I didn't know there was someone so eager to get in the sack with you!" said F, breaking the delicacy of the matter with a harsh laugh that trailed into a cough and ended with bits of his mucus deposited in the grass.

I denied this right away.

"Trust me, this has nothing to do with sacks—or getting into them."

F smiled comfortably to himself and turned back to his TV screen. "How goddamn romantic life can still be despite it all," he muttered, more to himself than to me.

"Oh, this has even *less* to do with romance," I answered back. "I only proposed to him because I need a father for my adopted child, and he only accepted because he needs to be married to a retard. See, no romance involved."

"Sure there is. Sure there is. You'll see."

OCTOBER 7

I T CAN be strange waking up and being eighteen one morning. But it doesn't necessarily have to be. Nothing is ever really very different when you turn a year older. You stumble out of bed like on any other day. Your eyelids are thick with sleep when you stare at yourself in the bathroom mirror, holding your toothbrush. Your cheeks are flushed from the blankets baking you all night. Your lips are dry, your skin pale, your hair looks like it's blowing in the wind. No difference from yesterday, when you were illegally smoking cigarettes.

I got out two elastic bands and began to braid my hair, a fat braid trailing from behind each ear, over my shoulders. I picked up the mascara and drove it carefully over my eyelashes until they were deep black and curved artificially up. I put on the only dress that was not in my dirty laundry basket—it happened to be a bright green, knitted dress that ended just above my knees, with short sleeves and a bow on the right shoulder made of crocheted string. Maybe it wasn't as appropriate as it could have been, but I wasn't about to do my laundry just because I was going to fill out a marriage certificate.

I pushed open my window and climbed out onto the roof. There was a part of the roof that dipped low over the garage and you could jump into the grass without serious injury; you'd just get up, brush your knees off, and walk away unnoticed. It was quite possibly the best feature our house had to offer. There was no other way of leaving the premises without "*Where are you going?*"

Fenton sat on a park bench, reading one of those thick books libraries buy only to fill up empty shelf space. I could never figure out why he bothered being so pretentious. Beside him lay a crinkled plastic bag and a yellow legal pad on which his right hand lay, armed restlessly with a pen.

I'd seen Fenton on and off at the library since we got "engaged," but we never mentioned October seventh. I really don't think we talked all that much—to be honest, there was no reason to talk. The fact that we were getting married was already settled and it was unlikely that either of us would have had second thoughts. Why would we reconsider? We didn't take it serious enough to reconsider. It was a way out, or a way in—or maybe it was just like a big fat piece of artificially colored candy. Neither of us really knew at the time what to expect, but whatever it might have been, it was the reason I walked to the library in a bright green dress on my birthday.

I stopped behind a tree and watched Fenton leaf through his book nervously, like he was desperately trying to find a specific paragraph. I was almost 300 percent certain that it would be safer to marry a plutonium bomb and romantically more satisfying to marry a screwdriver. But for some reason I believed it really wasn't so strange that we were marrying. I couldn't justify that thought, of course. I only knew that from all the people in town it was only this asshole I felt satisfied with. Satisfied? I didn't know what that meant either. It could have had something to do with the fact that we weren't strangers, and I guess there is something irreplaceable about familiarity. We had known each other from the library checkout line since I was about thirteen.

Five years ago. The first thing I ever said to him was:

"Are you renting those books out to prop open a door?"

He turned his head slowly and said, "No."

"Well, they look like they could suffocate someone."

Fenton's expression was sour far beyond his years. "Look, I'm not renting them out for *you*, so you're safe in your little world of *Seventeen* magazines."

I held a pile of books on goldfish in my hands and wasn't even aware that people seriously printed a magazine exclusively for seventeen-year-olds.

"And you're safe in your little world of *Behind the Scenes of the Modern Haiku*," I answered, "so we're both safe and sound."

The thing is I liked Fenton. I liked him the way that one would like an epileptic neighbor who throws fits on his front lawn every once in a while—and that emotion was more valid than the reasons most people come armed with when they step up to the altar. There was nothing wrong with this marriage. It was a decent match. Well, maybe "decent" isn't technically the correct word, but whatever. This would be one of those marriages made by some blacksmith in the underworld.

"Howdy," I said, sliding up next to Fenton on the bench.

His eyes remained on an underlined paragraph of the book in his lap. "Why do you always insist on using that weird cowboy greeting?" he asked.

"Actually it's a scientifically proven fact that not only cowboys use the expression."

"What's up with your dress?" he asked, gathering his things together.

"I don't know. You tell me."

"It's fucking green."

"It is. You gonna survive?"

"I'll *try*."

The sun beat down on us hard as we made our way to the parking lot. All the car tops glistened painfully, the trees seemed to play dead, and the apathetic department store customers staggered to their cars with hands clinging as though for life onto their plastic bags.

Fenton's strides were wide and impatient, leaving me forever to try and keep up. He was lost in his own dilemmas and ambitions every minute of the day. I had no way of breaking in. I'm not saying that I had any particular desire to break and enter into the holy sanctum that was Fentondom. All I'm saying is that it often would have made things more practical if sometimes we'd met somewhere on a bridge that connected our two caves. But that particular construction apparently just didn't exist. Our difficulties started with the way we chose to make use of our vocal cords. I had an uncontrollable habit of sowing comments, reading billboards out loud, and expressing random thoughts that wandered through my brain like aimless tourists—my mouth opened freely; his mouth only opened to spurt out shrapnel.

"Look at those slugs buying bargain country CDs at Wal-Mart. Why does everything about commercial life have to be so sad? This whole country is turning slowly into one large, stagnant pool of shoppers. It reminds me of that dried bacon fat, resting one inch deep at the bottom of an unwashed breakfast pan. God, it's hot—I feel like the inhabitant of a toaster."

Fenton glanced at me but restrained himself from speaking. I think he was trying to do me a favor. He stopped to pick up an old flyer that he found lying on the ground, and after scanning over it quickly he put it in his pocket and walked silently on. I was to find out soon that this was something he did all the time. He collected stuff like that. Third-rate pizza restaurants advertising their prices, gentlemen's clubs with names that made you want to roll your eyes into the back of your head, spa brochures with hard-to-make-out black-and-white pictures of mediocre-looking women smiling in bathing suits—all that kind of stuff.

Coming to a stop before a red Ford Taurus, Fenton began to fish for his keys. I put my hands behind my back and stared idly at an old camper that rose up behind him. Its aged side was painted a bad combination of yellow and brown. A rusted metal strip ran the length of the side and the windows were of that claustrophobic brown plastic that always looks stained with grease. It reminded me of bad air. One couldn't help but be impressed.

"I wish you owned that thing," I told him, nodding at the camper. "I've always wanted to be married to someone who owned a camper."

He turned toward me, surprised. "Did you think I owned this piece-of-shit red Ford car?"

"You're kidding," I muttered in awe.

"I *live* in that camper."

Well! I'd barely had time to utter my wishes, and some twisted fairy godmother was already making them a reality.

"And just so you know: I'd rather eat myself alive than drive a red car," he added gravely, sticking the keys into the camper door.

Somehow I didn't doubt it. Anyway, that was my introduction to Arlene. Yeah, I didn't think he was the kind of guy who named objects, but apparently he was. I realized soon enough that Fenton could not be Fenton without Arlene. Arlene was his goddess. Everything about her inspired in him that blind idolatry that teenage boys reserve for a particular girl's ass—and no matter what goodies might later come along their path, when they're eighty, they'll still swear on the welfare of the human race that there never was nor will be again anything as extraordinarily perfect as that girl's rear end. That's loyalty. Let nobody tell you that men have lost the ability for chivalrous worship. Even Fenton had his share of nobleness—of course it would take someone as "interesting" as he was to waste the entirety of it on a camper.

"Don't pull the door too hard when you open it—it only opens halfway. You'll bend it out of shape if you try to force it open any further. And if you slam it too hard, the rearview mirror falls off."

Fenton watched me anxiously as I followed his instructions. My earnest compliance eased his expression into neutral ground. For the first time in the history of our transactions it seemed I didn't give him a reason for loading a shotgun. He almost smiled as he started up the motor. And I almost smiled back.

At the county clerk's office we stood in a room that was the color of those operation garments that doctors wear on soap operas—when they throw critical glances at beautiful single mothers waiting to hear the fate of their child's burst appendix. We laid out our documents and signed our names while Darrel, a random stranger, acted as our witness. A month and three days later, our license was signed by the justice of the peace—and we walked out into the sunlight married. It was mid-November and the air was much cleaner than it had been all year. The humidity was leaving off just a bit, and a lot of the German tourists had evaporated. We walked down the steps of the county clerk's office like we'd done nothing more official than share a burger. Fenton was a few steps ahead of me, like always, and I hopped along after him. It was obvious that something in our behavior was lacking. Maybe a joke had to be cracked or a look had to be exchanged—something that would acknowledge the completion of this enormous and bizarre undertaking.

I began to laugh. I was Mrs. Flaherty after all, and that was a thought that seemed boundlessly silly and abstract. Fenton looked over at me the way he always did, and I winked at him. I don't think two human beings could have been more miserably matched and at the same time as satisfied as we were. "Fools," I believe is the technical term.

AIN'T NOBODY LOOKIN' NOW

DID I feel any different? Now that I was a married woman and had joined the billions of people who are glued to a mate—did something change? Did I gain the power to be sentimental—to sigh and become nervous, jealous, proud? People in magazines always looked like there was so much going on in their lives. As though there was nothing else about life except this enterprise—being attractive, being attract*ed*, having affairs, calling off affairs, or burning and melting into another human being in the true unification of love. They seemed to wallow in the complexities of their relationships. They seemed to live only to talk about its various, endlessly boring aspects to friends over lunches. The woes of love seemed to please them more than the summits of bliss—well, I guess everyone enjoys the advantages of being able to look sorrowfully down from a cross. I thought maybe the same would happen to me, and I braced myself for the worst, but I woke up the next day as childish as the day I was born.

Life continued to be ordinary. In fact, it was almost unusually ordinary, and inevitably I began to wonder whether I really did marry Fenton.

I made an appointment at the orphanage, and Fenton started on the novel in which I played the slow wife. Our meetings continued to be much the same as they had been up to then. The fact that the law had tied us together didn't make much of a difference to either of us, except that now when we ran into each other at the library we had an official reason to drift toward each other. Mainly we argued. God, we argued about everything under the sun, moon, and stars—even those things you couldn't rationally have found an aspect to argue about.

"It's obviously better to shower in the evenings than the mornings—no question about it," said Fenton.

"Obviously?"

"Yeah, obviously."

"Well, maybe you should start collecting signatures to pass a law about that, then."

"Look, for all I care, people can shower at three p.m. every second Sunday of the month. I'm only saying it's common sense to get into bed clean instead of sleeping with all the dirt you collected during the day. Now can you please go and bother someone else? I'm trying to concentrate."

"*You* started this conversation."

"Excuse me, *you* were the one who came over here and opened your mouth. I wouldn't have said anything to you at all."

"Well, you were the one who started talking about *showers*."

It was when January came around that I realized how Fenton had disappeared. I tried to remember the last time I had seen him, and all I could come up with was the thirteenth of December. I thought this over and realized I should probably be devastated. What can be worse to a young girl than the abandonment of a mate? Even when the mate wasn't a mate at all, but rather a poet marrying you for inspiration. Again, I felt like a malformation. I knew I ought to have locked myself in my room and cried for at least two weeks, and then, after that, continued to bear a mysterious burden wherever I went, so that people could whisper significant things about me (such as: "Don't mention *him* to her"). To have been burnt by love—that was no doubt the final destination of romanticism. Here I had the chance to make something tragic of my life, and I couldn't do it. Mourning over Fenton's absence seemed physically impossible. Quite frankly, I would have had an easier time writing a Nobel Prize–winning dissertation on olives.

If the earth had swallowed up my husband, then it must have had a good reason. I wasn't going to take this up with Mother Nature. Besides, having the library entirely to myself felt glorifying. I felt like the dog whose marked territory had finally been abandoned by an annoying neighborhood mutt. Or like the cowboy who, after uttering his famous line ("This town ain't big enough fer the both of us"), actually succeeded in driving away the enemy.

I lay back and decided to enjoy God's goodwill—little did I expect that it might very well be the devil's goodwill and that this particular gentleman's "goodwill" is always accompanied by an entourage of catastrophes. I didn't give this a second thought. The present was all that mattered in this whirlwind entitled "Hester's Life." I wasn't equipped with the paranoia to care about the dirty details of a distant future—about a disturbed look or a demand for an explanation that might take place somewhere in the folds of time. Trying to figure out how to dodge bullets that hadn't even been fired yet bored me.

I walked back into the orphanage, armed with documents declaring me a married eighteen-year-old woman. The fat lady, whose name I kept forgetting, like a goddamn curse, met me in her office much like the first time. I could see in her little restless eyes that she wasn't going to give me a kid no matter what. I was a burden on her precious time, and she had about as much interest in me as she would in a piece of toilet paper that refused to be flushed down the toilet. Needless to say, my confidence could have soared higher.

"Howdy," I said, and then I wished I hadn't said "Howdy."

"So you still want to adopt?" she asked, seating herself on the edge of her desk. It made me feel like I was in school again, trying to explain to the principal that aliens had abducted my homework.

"Yes, I still want to adopt."

"Hmm," she said, eyeing me. "You're really set on this?"

"You honestly think the urge to have a child is something that can be a one-week fad?"

"Mrs. Flaherty, I don't *think* anything. I just lay out the facts."

I flinched. I couldn't believe she called me Mrs. Flaherty. Suddenly I didn't feel like I was in the principal's office anymore. Actually, it was the first time in my whole *life* that I didn't feel like I was in the principal's office. I straightened myself up. It felt glorious being looked at as an adult—a little disconcerting, but glorious nonetheless. My words seemed to be weighted, as though now they deserved some attention. You see, for so many years, every time I talked, people looked at me like I was really just vomiting in a public space. Being called by a married name gave me back enough confidence to say just about anything.

"Well, lay 'em out," I said, referring to the facts.

She sighed. "I'll be honest with you. I don't think it's going to work."

"I thought you didn't *think*."

Her expression turned visibly sour. "We're going to have to process this information you filled out."

I leaned back and tilted my head, like an apathetic general watching his army run for their lives, while the sun casts the battlefield in heavy golden light.

"You're not going to accept me for adoption, will you?"

There was a tense pause. She got up from the desk and said, "No."

"Thanks. That's really all I wanted to know."

The town never looks good when dreams have been freshly shattered. It was late in the afternoon and now I'd have to try and figure out what bus connection I got home on the last occasion. I took a wrong bus again. You probably wouldn't think it to look at me, but I was devastated.

I had carefully built a whole little castle out of hope, and now it had an ax lodged in it. And now? Now I sat in a bus going down a wrong turn, with my thoughts digging holes into uncharted territory. And as though that wasn't bad enough, I was *married*. Not normal married. Married to Fenton Flaherty, who might have been dead for all I knew. It was a sad affair all around—my whole reason for being married to him in the first place had just been taken away from me by a fat lady who bore me some personal grudge.

It was past eight o'clock in the evening when I finally pushed open the front door. The aftermath of dinner was in full swing. I could hear dishes in the kitchen and loud talking. My mom was saying something about her menopause to someone else.

Having heard the door slam, she promptly appeared in the hall-way.

"Hester, where were you? You missed dinner."

I had given up telling lies a long time ago. It got to be too ar-duous, having to make up imaginary places and things you were doing every time you set foot in the driveway. I figured she didn't care anyway. It was just something she said.

"I was out at the orphanage. They won't let me adopt."

She turned back into the kitchen. "Well, Margaret is over with your uncle Norman and Jethro. I can't see why you need to pick *exactly* the day that they come over for dinner to be off some-where else."

"Sorry. I had no idea."

"Yeah, well, I'm afraid those kinds of excuses won't get you anywhere in life."

Uncle Norman, Margaret, Jethro. Never heard of them before. My parents had a vast family and we hardly knew any of them, but my mom liked to pretend we all grew up in the same neigh-borhood and had shared countless picnics, barbecues, and game nights.

I walked into the kitchen to shake hands with Margaret, who apparently was the second wife of Uncle Norman, who was my dad's older brother. Or something like that.

"Hello there," she said, smiling suspiciously.

Yeah, they'd been talking about me right before the meno-pause conversation.

"Hello there," I replied.

Margaret wore no makeup. She looked like she was a lumber-jack in her last lifetime. Her whole shape was large and stocky and kind of puffy around the face and arms and thighs. She wore her natural blond hair in a ponytail and khaki shorts with a T-shirt that said "Have a Good One!" on it. One of her hands was in her pocket and the other one was clasped around a cup of coffee.

"I heard a lot about you, Hester," she said, smiling like a toothpaste company was paying her for it.

"Oh, great."

"Your mom says you're interested in becoming a neurosurgeon."

"Yeah," I replied, "I'm either going into neurosurgery or professional surfing."

My mom looked over from the fridge with blatant distaste. "Hester, that's not funny."

I shrugged my shoulders and took a deep breath while Aunt Margaret stared on. She looked really healthy in that hiking type of way, but the strange thing is that it made her look desperately ill. It seemed that all that tanned skin, those freckles, and the healthy, blond ponytail was a sad facade for something worse than what my own mother was trying to hide. Suddenly I became nauseous like I hadn't been in a while. I clapped my hand in front of my mouth and muttered, "Excuse me, please."

"Where are you going?" my mother called.

"I think I'm going to throw up."

"Oh, for God's sake!"

I ran out while Margaret took a sip of her coffee, and my mother began to dissect me verbally without even having the grace of waiting until I was out of hearing range. I pushed open the bathroom door with my foot like in the movies and made for the toilet. Once I was done throwing up, I got to my feet and walked to the sink. My face was red and glazed in cold sweat, my eyes were sore and my eyelids swollen. I never cried when I was at my wit's end. I was at my wit's end far too often to indulge in tears, and so I only stared with wide eyes at myself in the mirror and thought: what a sad day when you realize that you can't get off the yellow brick road to neurosurgery—all you can do is *try*, and that is called floundering. You could try until the end of your days.

And that's when I swung open the door and found myself staring at a little obese kid with pitch-black olive eyes.

THE SECOND HONEYMOON

APPARENTLY MY uncle Norman married Margaret three years ago. Margaret was in his tennis club—or so the story goes. She was playing on the court next to his and before he knew it her tennis ball had broken his nose. Everything went from there. Uncle Norman is one of those helpless men who needs a large, fat mother to wipe the food from his mouth rather than a wife to walk around in high heels for him. Margaret was just that lady. She was the opposite of his first wife—she was the kind of woman who knew more about the garbage disposal than the plumber did. She knew what to do in case of a rattlesnake bite, she knew how to cook mediocre food with lots of protein in it, she knew how to wrestle a man to his knees who patted her ass, and she probably knew how to tackle a wild boar. She was part of the sailing club, the tennis club, and the Housing Committee for Legal Immigrants, and was also a loud singer in the front row of the local church choir.

Margaret was a monster rather than a human being. She was some kind of superpowered lawn mower or something.

She'd brought a small kid along to Uncle Norman's wedding from her first marriage to a Spanish commercial pilot. Jethro. He was seven at the time. Now, as Jethro stared at me from the other side of the bathroom doorway, he was ten. His black, greasy hair was sternly parted at one side and brushed over his head, like he was an old man trying to cover up a bald spot. His green-and-orange-striped T-shirt was tight around his stomach and stained in various places.

"Howdy," I said, stunned.

Jethro had eyes like torpedoes. Large, black, innocent, and powerful enough to convert you to any religion.

"Howdy," he answered back.

His skin was lacking the healthy glow one would expect from a well-fed Mediterranean lad. The olive shade of his face and arms had an unhealthy tint that almost bordered on purple.

"I'm Hester," I said.

"I'm Jethro."

We stood a while longer. For some reason it seemed we were supposed to have encountered each other in a more meaningful way. There were traces of the future to be smelled in the air, and it just seemed wrong that Jethro and Hester would run into each other over a bathroom doorway for the first time—I didn't know why. That's just the way it was.

"You done in there?" he asked eventually.

"Oh, yeah. Go ahead."

I walked down the hall to my room without turning to see if the little obese kid had been real or whether it was just a hallucination. I fell asleep thinking about college. Wondering whether I should give in or create some kind of Plan B. My eyes soon got heavy from thoughts that started out serious and melted into absurd dreamscapes, and I fell asleep draped over my chair, head in a book, hair over my desk.

Morning found me clambering out on the roof with a cigarette in my mouth and a lighter in my fist. I realized suddenly that the little obese kid from the night before had actually not been a remote hallucination. He was real. He was sitting out on the roof with a zebra-patterned sweater and antennas on his head made out of tinfoil.

Needless to say, I was pretty thrown off. I blinked and froze, not knowing whether to light my cigarette or take it out of my mouth and say something.

"Morning," he said, looking up from a pad on his lap.

"Morning."

His attention went back to his pad. My attention went to that intense pattern on his sweater. To call it fascinating would have been an understatement. It was downright hypnotic.

"What are you doing out here?" I asked, finally lighting my cigarette.

"Drawing a map of the neighborhood."

"Oh yeah? Why?"

"I need to find the best place for a landing platform."

"For what?"

"I'm building a spaceship."

"Oh."

God, I wished all conversations could be this simple.

"Jethro, right?" I asked.

"Yeah," he said, not taking his eyes off the pad.

"Well, that sounds interesting, Jethro. To be honest, it's probably the most interesting project I've heard of in a long time."

He looked up with a helpless smile, and I could tell he had

been waiting to hear something like that all his life. It was kind of disturbing. And Lord knows it was too early for sad scenes like this. But Jethro was now on a roll. His eyes cleared into huge marbles, glowing with delight.

"I'm going to become an astronaut when I grow up," he offered up.

"Yeah, I can tell."

"You can tell?"

"Of course I can tell."

"How?"

"Well," I said, "you're sitting out here at eight thirty in the morning making maps of the neighborhood to build a landing platform for your spaceship. That's a pretty goddamn promising start."

He seemed satisfied with my explanation and went back to work with a subtle smile that couldn't have been sucked off his face with a vacuum cleaner. And I leaned back, my eyelids still full from sleep, proud that somewhere and somehow I was able to put a smile on a little kid's face.

"So you guys are staying for the weekend or something?" I asked.

"No, my mom went to Hawaii with Norman on a second honeymoon. They're coming back to get me in two weeks."

That made me wonder what in her right mind would make my mother take in some relative's kid for two weeks. There were obviously other reasons involved—too hard for the little kid to know. I asked my mom later that day.

"Mom, Margaret has a tumor or something, right? Or she's getting an abortion."

She looked over from the sofa. "Hester, what are you talking about?"

"I mean, there has to be a *real* reason why they dropped their kid off here for two weeks."

"They're on a honeymoon."

"But—who takes a honeymoon three years into their marriage?"

"Hester, please!" She muted the television to give me her full attention. "Why can't you stop being such a pain in the ass? Go and do something normal for a change. Do whatever it is kids your age are supposed to be doing this time of the year."

I was at a loss for words, and instead of answering her I wondered desperately why I started conversations with my mother in the first place.

"It's about high time you got yourself a boyfriend, by the way," she added before she turned the sound back on.

Technically I would be cheating on my husband if I did that.

She muted the screen again with a new thought: "Why don't you ask Hannah if she'll take you along to one of those get-togethers she's always going to?"

Well, probably because I'd rather clean out a Porta Potti with my tongue.

Then she began looking annoyed and kind of constipated. "Why don't you ever answer me when I say something?"

"Sorry," I said, running a cold hand over my forehead. "My train of thoughts had a collision."

She turned away from me and switched the sound back on the television for the second time.

"Honey, there's something wrong with you. There really is."

Regardless of whether there was something wrong with me or not, I now had a little brother who got up at the crack of dawn every morning and could be found in the backyard most of the day, building a spaceship. And when he went to bed at night he had bizarre dreams of conquering planets in distant galaxies that had rivers of chocolate—sometimes he'd also have dreams of sailing the Caribbean on a pirate ship, but that was the more rare dream. Mostly he dreamed of those chocolate rivers—exactly in the way that old homeless men dream of whiskey rivers.

Jethro was mostly quiet. I was far more hyperactive than he was. His answers were short and usually completely unaffected by anything. Not that he was cold, because he wasn't. He was just a little kid who would make no pretenses in interest, fascination, or understanding unless there was any cause for it. He wasn't easy to shake up and his imagination seemed to take good care of him. What I mean is that he didn't need much, because he thrived so perfectly on the things he thought up and laid out for his future. He was dreaming constantly—during the night, during the day, during lunch, dinner, and breakfast—and even when you talked to him you could see that each word triggered new explosions behind his head and that pictures, sounds, colors, and smells were washing in and out of one another, constantly creating new scenes. Jethro was blessed with a flawless imagination. Of course Hannah had already diagnosed him with three different psychological ailments by the time we had dinner on the first day.

Speaking of which, it was a strange sight to see someone new at the dinner table squeezed in between Hester and Hannah. My mother smiled and made some comment about bread sticks. My dad said a few sentences about the stock market, but mainly it was Hannah talking. As a general rule: it's next to impossible to shut my sister up. She'd always trample over everything and talk about whatever you least wanted to hear just then. As for me, I sometimes even forgot that I was sitting at the table. Mainly I just ate and turned thoughts over in my head, where no one could see them. I tried my best not to talk in front of my family. I hated the conversations that we had, and I hardly ever understood what we were talking about anyway—especially at dinner. So I opened my mouth only when it was absolutely imperative: "Hannah, I think it's really detrimental to your health the way you keep your head up your own asshole—you should pull it out sometime and take a breath."

To which my mother would put down her fork and look over at her husband. "Richard, *you* talk to her!"

And my dad would say, mechanically and bored: "Hester, that's really unacceptable language at dinner."

And I'd say, "Yeah, I know." And maybe I'd smile and add, "But we all agree, right?"

"Fuck you, Hester!" That would be my sister.

And then my mother would say something about the language again, and eventually someone would stand up, chair flying out behind them, and desert the dining room. Usually Hannah would be the first. By the time the curtain fell on the deserted dinner scene, there would just be me sitting there, wishing we could all be pigeons and lead peaceful lives. Dinner never once swerved from this pattern, until that night when Jethro and I first sat alone at the table together.

IF IT KEEPS ON RAINING

I STILL DON'T know exactly how it happened, but before I knew it I was out in the garage helping Jethro tape his cardboard space-ship together on a regular basis. We learned all about aerody-namics and I even stole my mother's credit card to pay off my library bills so that we could rent a shitload of books on galaxies and NASA and whatnot.

At night I'd be looking up at my bedroom ceiling, smiling. It had been ages since I last used my time so wisely. Ages since I woke up in the morning with utter disregard for the plastic surgery being performed on my future. It seemed there wasn't even time to look for hope and wonder if things would turn out "all right" anymore—there was a spaceship to be built, there was the whole neighborhood to map out in a three-color code on cardboard, there was the library bill to hide from my mom, and then there was the problem of building a landing platform in the neighbor's concrete backyard without them noticing.

I was eighteen years old, on the brink of tipping over into some stupid disaster that would glue me to a pattern until the end of my life. The water was rising, and I couldn't really afford *not* to be paranoid. So why was I renting out books from the library about astronomy with a fat kid? I don't know. Probably because I could talk to the fat kid like I used to talk in my playground days to Mark—without feeling like some cop car's lights were freezing me in a stolen vehicle without registration.

Jethro looked so innocent and naive, like he was lost among the acid characteristics of the human race; but if you looked closely, an expression would flitter across his features once in a while that betrayed a hidden intelligence sharp enough to cut through an iron vault door.

He didn't eat a lot, like the cliché for round kids goes. In fact, I'd even go so far as to say he *disliked* food. He hardly ever ate at meals. Jethro ate like a heroin addict—with a shameless sweet tooth and a bad habit of making himself an awful lot of instant coffee when the kitchen was deserted. I walked in on him once while he was in the middle of pouring the hot water into his cup. He froze for a second, then took out a spoon and began to study me carefully as he stirred his coffee.

"My mom would kill me if she knew I was drinking coffee," he said solemnly.

"Well," I said, "she better not find out, then."

"You won't tell her?"

"No. I happen to believe that everyone has a right to ruin their health if they want to."

He smiled, pleased.

"Here, I got you a book on frog anatomy at the library," I said, placing a massive picture book on the kitchen table.

"Thanks."

We both dropped our eyes to the glossy cover, where a brilliant, green frog stared back at us.

"Why'd you get me a book on frogs?"

"Because it's amazing, Jethro. Take a look—maybe you wanna just skip page thirteen, though."

"Why?"

"Because it shows frogs . . . it shows them . . . well, you know what I'm talking about—they're trying to have a baby frog."

He stared wordlessly at me, and I wondered why I mentioned it in the first place. He probably never would have figured out what was going on in the picture anyway.

"Look, Jethro," I began, glancing suspiciously toward the doorway, "you might find this hard to believe, but all those stories about storks 'n shit delivering babies to parents' doorsteps just because they held hands and wished for a kid—well, they're not true."

For a while it looked like he wasn't going to say anything, and I began to feel uncomfortable and wondered whether I had just pulled the base of his whole reasoning from underneath his feet. I got that sinking-stomach feeling that you get when you've just permanently traumatized a child.

Then he said, "What are you talking about?"

"Never mind," I said, patting him on the back, "I guess you escaped the mass brainwashing."

"Heck, I know how all that stuff really works."

"You do, huh?"

"Figured it out years ago," he said with schoolyard pride.

I was considerably surprised, because *I* never knew what the hell went on in nature until I was about sixteen, and even then most of what I knew belonged in a science-fiction book rather than a textbook on human biology.

"Well, that's impressive, Jethro," I said.

He shrugged his shoulders. "Babies are made from spit. It's pretty obvious."

Hmm.

"Well," I said, "let's just say it's a *kind* of spit."

My mother hated the way I spent time with Jethro. She said I wasn't "developing" right and that something was wrong with me. I said, "Didn't we figure that out a long time ago?" Then she said she didn't want to see me playing with toys in the garage anymore, and I said I was building a spaceship, not playing with toys. She looked at me like I had a noodle stuck across my cheek in a fancy restaurant.

"You only have two more weeks until your college interview. Do you realize what it took for the school to even *consider* accepting you this late?"

"Sure."

"You obviously don't have a clue."

I didn't. And to be honest: I'd be darned if I cared.

"Hester, I'm not going to let you disappoint us. You might as well know that. You're going to go make it into that goddamn college and then into university—even if I have to bribe every governor in every state."

Well, I realized she was kind of set on the whole Hester-the-brain-surgeon fantasy. And I wasn't about to take anybody's fantasy away from them.

"Okay, Mom."

She looked at me straight, and time seemed to stop. I hated when that happened. It always left me swimming in a vast void. Plus, it made me think too much about where to put my hands.

"I said *okay*, Mom."

"Hmm," she said, turning around, "that's what I'm worried about, quite frankly."

I sighed. "Look, I said okay. I'll study. What more do you want? A legal document with the date and my signature?"

"I want you married to someone who isn't a plumber or a lawn mower for a living or has a mullet, don't you understand that?"

"They have a course for that in college?"

Her eyes couldn't have been more deadly. "I don't appreciate sarcasm, Hester. And I believe you know that."

"Yeah, I believe I do. But just so you know: *technically* that was more of a joke rather than straight-up sarcasm. I think if I wanted to be an asshole I would have said something on the order of—"

"Stop that!" she said, waving an irritated hand through the air. "I am trying to give you a decent life here, Hester, and you're acting like that means *nothing*. I'm trying to give you what all these thousands of Mexicans dream of when they try and hop the border!"

"Well, I appreciate that," I said.

And I guess in a way I was telling the truth. I did appreciate the crude and completely automated mother-bear intentions behind her makeup-plastered face. She meant good. No doubt. And the example she made with the Mexican dreams of America almost made the whole conversation worthwhile. Not that I was actually going to study now, but at least I'd *tell* her I'd study now. I tried to be honest most of the time—painfully honest, suicidally honest—but there comes a time when all honesty is in vain, and you just want to lie about studying to get into college to meet illustrious men who don't have mullets. You just wanna say okay to everything and then do the opposite.

"I guess one good thing about going to college is that I get to pack my bags."

I was walking with Jethro down the sun-drenched winter-morning streets. The library loomed in the distance and we were just about to cut through the park.

Jethro kept his eyes on the road and answered, "Why the heck do you need to wait to go to college to pack your bags?"

"I don't know," I said, with a smile that made me feel like a fool. "I'm sure there's a reason."

He raised his eyebrows at me, but didn't say anything. And neither did I, because it was obvious that he'd won the battle. Then he took off running, and I called after him that I'd meet him at the checkout counter in two hours.

The library smelled of rusty radiator and patched-up heating systems. It was cold outside now—or at least it was cold enough for Floridians to scrape sweaters from boxes at the back of their closets. All the bums now sat inside, rather than lying under the palm trees. They sat slumped over tables reading everything from colorful entertainment magazines to textbooks on computer programming. A bunch of overweight people occupied the computers. A school class of seventh graders were scattered through the biography section with notepads—most of them laughing and passing notes over their books. Other than that, the library was of course empty. I squeezed myself into a far corner and, surrounded by books on religion, pulled out something about Buddhism. I must have stared for fifteen minutes at an old illustration of Buddha sitting under the Bodhi tree.

"On the night of the full moon, after overcoming the attacks and temptations of Mara, 'the evil one,' he reached enlightenment, becoming a Buddha at the age of 35."

My gaze wandered from the page for reasons unknown, and I found myself staring at a pair of worn-out black shoes with the torn hem of black pants resting on them.

There wasn't even time to think "Oh, shit." My stomach went climbing up my throat. I didn't want to look up any farther, but freezing for eternity wasn't an option. So, slowly I let my eyes crawl on up as I sat there on the floor, with my legs lifelessly outstretched and the sunlight draping bright strips of light over them.

All his mythological features were back in sharp focus, an inch before my face. The right eye that was slightly lazy—just the sort of physical abnormality that seems too perfect to be a natural defect. In my opinion it was the only thing that made it possible to look at Fenton's face at all.

He stared at me as distantly as the day we first struck up conversation; the only difference was that his winter clothes were now appropriate. His face was slightly tanned and his chin was covered with the beginnings of a beard. It looked like he was on the verge of accidentally transforming into a hippie.

With his hands in his pockets and his eyes locked unflinchingly on my own, we seemed to stare at each other for a whole lifetime. I mean, what do you say? What are you supposed to say when your husband one day crashes through some barn's roof and lands right there in the haystack in front of you with an unchanged expression?

ONE DAY, ONE DAY

FENTON SHIFTED his weight uncomfortably, hands in his pockets, a little defensive.

"*What?*" he asked.

"Nothing," I said.

"What do you mean 'nothing'?"

"I mean 'nothing.'"

He rolled his eyes. "You obviously *don't* mean 'nothing.'"

"I do. I happen to be blank right now."

"Look, I've lived with enough women to know that they aren't ever thinking 'nothing.'"

"Glad to know you're a professor of the female psyche, but I guarantee you if you x-rayed my head right now, you'd find a lonesome tumbleweed blowing over a vast nothingness. And if you wanna take that down in your notebook as 'highly unusual behavior,' go right ahead."

He stood back, visibly disappointed that there were no treasure troves to be discovered. It can sometimes be hard in the expectance of drama to be left with nothing. No handle to grab hold of. No thread to go along with. I figured I better help him out.

"So, where have you been anyway?" I asked.

"I was in Europe. Hiking. In Switzerland."

"Why?"

"Because I *was*."

Oh, well didn't the light just shine through the dark clouds and clear up everything!

"You're such an egotistical asshole—I'm really impressed," I said, getting up off the floor.

"Is that a compliment?"

"Sure. Life's too short not to take everything as a compliment."

He didn't say anything.

"Look, I don't even care about you being an asshole and all. If you have the sudden urge to climb mountains in Europe, I wouldn't dream of stopping you, just so you know."

He looked at me seriously. "We both knew this wasn't going to be a normal marriage."

"Fenton, the only thing in the *universe* I know right now is that this marriage isn't normal."

"So why are you all pissed, then?"

"I'm not! I just told you I don't care. I don't even care that you didn't *tell* me about your Swiss disappearing act until now."

"The reason I didn't tell you about the trip was because I didn't feel like being on a fucking radar screen."

"Honey, I'm with you all the way on that one. If there's one thing I don't want, it's you on my radar screen. Trust me. We see eye-to-eye on this."

Who knows if he was even listening? I had a feeling that half the things I said to him were lost to some alternate universe. He had this way of freezing in time and space, looking out at me as though from inside a large ice cube. I would have given my right arm to know what he was thinking half the time.

"Oh, another thing," he said. "Just because you're probably going to wonder about this later anyway: *yes,* I had affairs over there with women."

I guess it was as honest a comment as I could ask for, even though I hadn't asked for it.

"What makes you think I would wonder about that?"

"Because you're acting like a *wife,*" he said.

"If I were acting like a wife, you'd have a lawsuit on your hands, and half your camper would be mine before you knew what hit you. If anyone is playing house here it's *you,* acting like a goddamn husband, going off without a word, having affairs with women in Europe."

"I thought we were both fine with that."

"We *are* both fine with that! I'm just making a point. Never mind! You know, I don't think we even have the legal right to argue about our marriage. It's nothing more than a bit of paperwork filed away in some office. It's not even a green-card marriage. It's nothing. So can we please avoid this boring subject in the future, and stop pretending like we even care?"

"I was just being practical. I'm letting you know all this now, so that it won't be an issue later."

"Well, I appreciate that, Fenton," I said, putting my hand on his shoulder, "but as much as you'd like to think I give a shit about your sex life, I don't. So there is no need to beat around the bush—or to not beat around the bush."

Fenton let out some kind of cough and said, "Well, whatever. I have to go have lunch with my dad—it's his birthday today."

Boy, just when you're sure someone was conceived in a test tube you find out they have parents. He turned to leave, and when he was about halfway down the narrow passage of the shelving system I called after him.

"Wait, can I ask you something?"

He stopped and looked immediately annoyed. "If it were up to me, no, but I guess there's freedom of speech and all that."

"I was wondering why the hell you live in a camper—I mean if you have a dad. You might even have a mom, I don't know."

"I can't have a dad and a camper at the same time?"

"Well, it's not illegal, it's just kinda weird. Why do you live in a camper instead of with your family?"

"I'm twenty-one. Old enough to drink, gamble, smoke, and own a camper."

"Okay, fine. Just thought I'd ask if there's anything really weird going on that I should be aware of. I don't know, maybe your family is part of the Mafia or something. The Mafia families all live in Florida, you know. That's why they have all those Italian delicatessen stores around."

"Unless there's a Swedish Mafia, I think you can rule that one out."

I had forgotten about his straw-blond hair and blue eyes for a second. "I was just making a point, Fenton," I said, shrugging my shoulders. "If you're hell-bent on being a mysterious weirdo, then don't let me take that away from you. I don't want to ruin your image or anything."

Fenton sighed. "What is it with you?"

"Nothing. I just thought since we're being all honest and straightforward today I'd use the opportunity to find out if there's any creepy history of yours I should know about. There could be, you know. That's all."

He rolled his eyes. "My mom remarried when I was five. She lives in Oregon with her new husband and kids. My dad's an accountant. He lives a few blocks away from here and the reason I moved out into a camper three years ago is—well, *you* have parents. You should know."

I nodded. "Yeah, I do."

And he disappeared.

A strong wind began to sweep through the streets as Jethro and I started on our way home that afternoon. The sky was cluttered with wild clouds, and where it shimmered through the branches of swaying trees the sky glowed in a pale green color that somehow didn't seem to belong in the sky.

"Something is brewing at home," I said uneasily, glaring at the sky.

"How do you know?" Jethro asked.

"I can tell by the weather."

His eyes grew big. "You can tell the future by the weather?"

"It's the most accurate way to go about it if you ask me."

"That doesn't make any sense."

"Romantic days like these were made for drama, Jethro. This is the perfect setting for tragedy—or black comedy."

We walked on slowly, and then he said, "Well, I don't believe in telling the future. I think the future just comes by itself."

"I'm not asking you to believe in anything. I'm just stating a fact here: there's some kinda trouble going on at home, and I have a feeling it's not going to properly kick off until I get there, because I'm probably the main ingredient."

"Well, what should we do?" he asked, a little worried despite his alleged disbelief.

"We throw open the front door and walk right into it."

"Why would you walk right into it if you know it's going to be bad?"

"Because I'm curious, Jethro. Curiosity always gets the best of me."

"Well, can't you sneak around the back and find out?"

"Sure, but then I'd wonder for the rest of my life what would have happened if I had thrown open the front door and just waltzed in."

Jethro waved me off. "You're weird."

"So they say."

We approached the house like it was a huge time bomb. It looked peaceful enough from the outside, but that throbbing green sky was still hanging over it, and there was a plastic bag crawling over the driveway in the wind. There's a lot you can tell by lonely plastic bags on windy days. We crossed the porch, unlocked the door, and threw it wide open. For a matter of seconds we just stood there, waiting for whatever would decide to happen. And then Hannah stepped into the hallway from the kitchen. When she saw me, she stopped and grinned helplessly.

"Holy shit, Hester. Holy *shit*," she said, shaking her head slowly.

"Is that Hester?" I heard my mom's voice come unsteadily from the kitchen.

My sister told her "yeah" and then, turning back to me, said, "I think mom wants you."

My mother was sitting at the kitchen table with the phone and a mountain of used tissues scattered around her. Her makeup was smeared together with mascara and tears, and everything had dried halfway, so that her face looked like it was slowly sliding down south. When she saw me standing in the doorway her left eye began to twitch. She had a hard time keeping her body under any kind of control when she was emotionally taxed. I just stood there and wondered when she was going to open her mouth and say it.

"What?" I asked eventually. "What is it? Is anybody going to let me in on what I did?"

Her eyelids were bright red and her eyes bloodshot, but her hair was styled with immaculate mediocrity. As far back as I can remember she always had that indestructible news-reporter-lady hairstyle. Not a strand out of place.

"I don't know," she said, her voice dramatically quivering. "I really don't know if I can have this conversation with you right now, Hester. Or should I say *Mrs. Flaherty!*"

I could feel myself wanting to give in to gravity and barely managed to put my hand out to the door behind me for balance. Feeling the doorknob, I fondled the thought of rushing out into the green afternoon, jumping over the fence with an elaborate movement, and disappearing forever. But on second thought, I decided there really couldn't be anything more interesting than what might possibly happen next. That's one problem I've always had: when I'm anywhere up shit creek, I have to know how far up that creek actually goes.

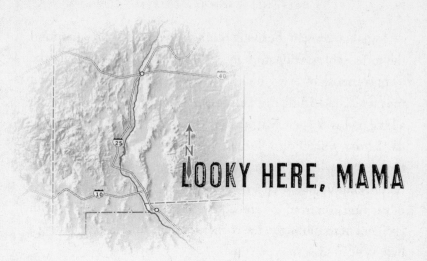

LOOKY HERE, MAMA

I GUESS IF you get married secretly to poets who want to use you for literary material, you'd better dedicate a minute to think of what you'd say if your parents ever found out. I never thought of it. Frankly, people have had more meaningful enemas than this marriage, so why would I even have contemplated telling my parents? Telling my parents about this marriage seemed like such a sad, sad joke. But you're lost in this world if you don't have backup plans, safety nets, and lies to save your ass when the time comes. The time always comes. I forgot this little fact all too often. The time comes, and you find yourself on your knees, frantically trying to clean up a mess that spreads all the way to the horizon. And of course everything that comes out of your mouth is officially the wrong thing to have said. It echoes after you in the room and stings, and leaves you wishing you could crawl back into the womb you came from, shrink back to the size of a single cell, and dissolve into nothingness.

"Listen—people have had more meaningful enemas than this marriage."

I was standing in the living room. My whole family sat around the coffee table staring up at me with anticipation, waiting for me to make sense of everything. My marriage license was lying on the table. Dr. Griffith, our family counselor, sat opposite me, with a legal pad and a pen. My mother hadn't stopped crying since the day before, when I came home from the library and found her in the kitchen with all the tissues. My dad was bored and irritated that his family had such a talent for creating abnormal methods of keeping him from the golf course. Hannah sat beside him with excitement trembling in the corners of her eyes. She was having a ball. Well, at least *someone* was.

"Hester," Dr. Griffith said, "why do you choose to use the word 'enema' to describe your marriage?"

"I don't know," I said, wiping the cold sweat from my forehead. "I was just trying to make a point. If I was going to take an enema, would I parade the news through town? No. Same with the marriage. It's not the kind of thing you send a newsletter about. I—I just didn't think it was necessary to mention it. I didn't think anyone would be interested in knowing."

"Oh, that's rich!" my mother cried out suddenly, bringing her fist down on the coffee table. "That's just rich!"

And maybe it *was* rich. Who knows? All I really knew was that I couldn't breathe anymore in that room. I wished for once I could just pass out and see black. Maybe fall into a coma for thirty years and wake up when everyone else was dead . . . but I've never had that kind of luck. Everything was in sharp focus. I could hear the breathing of every pair of lungs, I could hear the ticking of the clock in the kitchen, I could hear the sweat trickling down armpits and the television sets blaring all down the block.

"Hester, I think we need to know a little more here," Dr. Griffith said, trying to smile.

"I thought my point was pretty all-inclusive."

"I'm not saying that it wasn't. But we're going to need you to open up a little more, okay? Can you help us out with that?"

"Probably not," I said sincerely. "Anyway, isn't it time to ask someone else a question?"

"Well, I'm afraid you're the only one here who can let us know about all those feelings you keep locked up. Nobody else can do that for you."

I looked at Dr. Griffith like I was witnessing a bad accident with a bulldozer.

"Hester, will you just please answer the question!" my father said.

"I'm sorry, I don't have—feelings 'locked up,'" I said. "The only feeling I have right now is nausea, and I think it's plastered all over my face in broad daylight."

"That's not a feeling," my sister cut in. "That's a physical condition."

I closed my eyes and with every last scrap of energy that I had in my possession, I managed not to knock her head against the corner of the glass coffee table. I didn't even flinch.

Then I opened my eyes and said, "Fact is, I could talk for three days, and I swear to God none of you would have understood any part of what I said. And I might add that you all know that. What I don't understand is why we bother with this whole ordeal every time someone slams his finger in a door. I think it's high time we realize we don't give a shit about each other anyway. Nobody cares! We couldn't give a damn even if we *tried*. And if you think about it, we're blessed. If we really took advantage of our dysfunctional qualities we could be so god-damn carefree!"

Everyone remained silent with muscles strained painfully, ready to jump from their seats and fire semiautomatic weapons. The only reason we behaved ourselves at all was because of the balding shrink.

"Sorry, I didn't mean to say 'shit,'" I added in my usual clumsy aftermath of regret.

"Why do you have to be so hurtful, Hester?" my mother cried.

"I don't know, I guess it comes natural—I'm not really trying at all."

"How can you treat me like this? Do you realize that I gave up nine months out of my life so that I could give birth to you? Nine months. How much blood, sweat, and tears I've dedicated to producing you? And then you marry secretly and leave me out of your life like this? Don't you think you've done enough?"

I just stared at her performance. I admit I had no compassion left. At this point, I wouldn't have been able to stoop down and save a bunny from being blown off the face of the earth by one of those certified villains that are always around in storybooks and cartoons. I was milked dry. I wanted to be on some Australian mountain range, but unfortunately I was in the middle of my parents' living room. What's worse, there was a small audience looking up at me, ready for my monologue, and I had no choice but to give it to them.

"I didn't realize getting married was a felony. If I knew, I would probably have taken more precautions to hide the certificate. But I don't regret the whole marriage thing, if that's what you're after. I wish I could tell you I did—we'd probably all be out of here a lot faster—but all I can really say is I'm sorry my marriage is giving you the same symptoms as really bad food poisoning. I've been there before and it's not fun. I guess I'm actually sorry about that."

My mother's eyes darted up at me with a wild glare. "Oh, I'm glad you *guess* that you're sorry. That just takes care of everything, doesn't it? *Glory hallelujah!* Why don't we all just have a party and get drunk in order to celebrate the fact that you guess you're sorry!"

Then she started crying again. I thought it was pretty obvious that we were going in circles, but Dr. Griffith thought otherwise.

"Good. That's good. We're getting somewhere here. Hester, how does your mother's reaction make you feel?"

"Deeply cleansed," I said with a half-assed smile.

And did I mention I had a black eye? A toaster collided with my face the day before. My mom had meant to aim the toaster at the wall right beside me, but the tears clogging her eyes brought about a little miscalculation. Or so she said. After I had fallen through the doorway and hit the floor, she looked up for a second and blurted out: "Wonderful! Now look what you've done! Standing in the way like that—your face is probably going to be permanently deformed now and you'll never get anywhere at all!"

We were now only fifteen minutes into the counseling session. Fifteen minutes and already I felt like I'd been in hell long enough to ask the devil if eternity was over. I honestly didn't know how I would last the rest of the hour in this room. What with the bruise around my left eye flaming into red, swollen pain, the nausea, the heat, and the idea that we were going to spend more time talking about why I married Fenton. So, I did what one does in such situations.

"Can I use the bathroom?"

Hannah rolled her eyes. "She's just trying to get out of here, Dr. Griffith."

"Are you just trying to get out of here, Hester?" he asked.

"No. I need to use the bathroom."

"Christ!" my father muttered. "We're never going to get anywhere at this rate."

"You're just saying that so you can go back to your game!" my mother wailed. "None of us matter to you, do we?"

(Hadn't I tried to make that point earlier?)

"Excuse me," I said, discreetly making for the door.

I crawled up the stairs and swung open the door to the guest room, where Jethro lay spread out on his bed with a mountain of comic books. He looked up.

"How's it going down there?" he asked.

"I came to say good-bye. I'm leaving. And if I ever come back here, it'll be because somebody ran me over accidentally and this was the only address they found in my wallet."

"Where are you going to?"

"I don't know."

"Can I come?"

"Honey, I'm going forever."

"Yeah, I know."

This was the part where I was supposed to choke up and convince him that it would be safer if he stayed and waited for his mother to get back from Hawaii with Uncle Norman. I was supposed to tell him that this was no life for a little kid. This was too risky. I was supposed to throw my arms around him and wish him luck and say that maybe one day we'd run into each other again.

"Jethro," I said solemnly, "if you can pack fast enough, you can come."

He jumped off his bed immediately and began by scooping all his comic books into a plastic bag.

I ran across the hall to my room and scanned over my belongings. I figured I had about forty-five seconds left before somebody would come up the stairs and knock on the bathroom door. Packing under time pressure was never my forte. I would have rather packed nothing at all, but I couldn't do that either. This was my permanent departure from eighteen years of my life; it would have been highly unromantic and probably illegal to leave with nothing at all. So I climbed onto my bed and took the Ronald Peterson degree off the wall. I threw on my coat, scarf, and hat and grabbed a few extra dresses and two random library books. Just as I opened the window, Jethro came running through the doorway with his suitcase and the bag of comic books. We didn't say anything. Just climbed out the window, crawled over the roof, and jumped into the grass around the back of the house.

BIG FAT MOON

THAT EVENING at eight I sat on a park bench with a cigarette between my fingers. It was burning low, and I continued to suck at it nervously. I wasn't nervous for any of the right reasons, but I was nervous all the same. My stomach was turning somersaults. I didn't really know why exactly I was uneasy—all I knew was that my hand trembled when I held it up, and my head gave me no peace of mind. Thoughts just barged in and out like they didn't know any better. No closing the doors behind them.

I looked at the tobacco glowing between my white fingers and wondered about whether I'd soon run out of money to buy cigarettes—how would it feel wanting nicotine and not having the money to buy it? But I didn't worry about it yet. Most likely, it would only make the sensation of smoking more powerful.

It had rained briefly and my hair hung over my ears in wet, glossy streaks. Jethro was at a twenty-four-hour general store across the street. I had told him to wait there, because I had a delicate matter to take care of. Beside me lay my belongings—two books, Ronald Peterson's high school diploma, and some clothes I'd brought. The romantic afternoon morphed into a romantic evening. I finished another cigarette and then began to read some pointers on how to knit patterns into sweaters. That's when Fenton showed up. He threw himself onto the far side of the bench and looked over, uninspired.

"What's wrong with your face?" he asked.

"A toaster hit me."

"Toasters don't usually do that kind of thing," he said.

"It's a long story—mind if I start at the beginning?"

I could already see the dread in his eyes.

"I don't know," he said. "Do I *want* to hear the story?"

"Yeah, you probably do."

"I probably don't."

"Okay, you probably don't, but we all have to listen to stories we don't wanna hear at some point or another, so just pull yourself together. You might just survive this."

Fenton raised his eyebrows condescendingly, but kept his mouth shut.

"Well," I began carefully, "you know how I lived with my parents?"

"Yeah . . . ?"

I applied the cigarette to my lips. "Our marriage is out in the open. They know."

"Who's 'they'?"

"Everyone has a 'they.' 'They' are the people that look at you weird. They're the ones always loading up custom-made shotguns behind bushes. They're the reason you look over your shoulders. In my case, it's the family. My mom found out about the marriage, threw a toaster in my face, and next thing I know I take a bathroom break in a family counseling session and climb out my bedroom window. And here I am."

There was a short pause. Fenton's eyes remained blinkless in irritation. Wide, disturbed, and beautifully blue.

"So . . . I'm sorry—is that positive or negative?"

I smiled. "It's very positive."

"Why?"

"Because I'm not going back."

"What do you mean, you're not going back?"

"I'm not going back means I'm not going back. I resigned my position as family mushroom."

"So you ran away from home, huh?"

"I climbed out the window. No running involved."

He looked at me, annoyed.

"You ran *away*," he repeated emphatically and slowly. "Just like some sixteen-year-old brat who's pissed at her parents for not buying her a BMW."

Fenton had a talent for talking out of his ass, but it didn't catch me by surprise anymore. I just shrugged my shoulders.

"I left—that's all that matters. *How* I left doesn't make a difference. Sure, I could have left like a sixteen-year-old brat who wanted a BMW, or a senior citizen who wants to go out with a bang; I could have left like a plumber who did a lousy job—or the mailman who came for other reasons than to deliver mail. I could even have left like an eighteen-year-old married kid who just got a prescription for Prozac. I could have left any old way, Fenton. All that really matters is that I *left*."

"Hester, you're not in a movie. You can't just grab your popcorn and walk out when you're bored."

"Really?"

"Yeah, so spare me the monologues."

Fenton's stare remained unaltered, although there were hints of his wit's end visible in the red net of capillaries stretching over his eyeballs. He slammed the newspaper he had carried under his arm hard against the park bench.

"Fenton," I said, "why don't you stop beating around the bush and tell me what you really wanna say. I know what it is anyway."

He looked up. "Okay, fine: *You're not moving into the camper with me.*"

It took him long enough, but at least now that it was verbally established, I could work at eroding his resolution. He already looked a little guilt-stricken. Like a small, pale conscience was denting his asshole aura in some minor way. It actually made him seem adorable.

"I can't live with anyone. I need to be alone—I can't work with someone around, and my life depends on my work. So basically if you move in, I'm fucked."

I just smiled.

"If I can't write, then I might as well slit my wrists right now," he continued. "You understand? I wasn't born to get married and go to PTA meetings and fill out tax forms. You have to go back home."

"Really?"

"Hester, I'm serious. I can't take you into the camper, and that's final. Nothing you're going to say will change that, so you might as well grab that weird little pile of clothes you brought and get your ass back home."

I put my hand trustingly on his shoulder. "Now listen: you not wanting to go to PTA meetings is one thing, but I'm afraid nowhere along the line did you acquire the authority to tell me where to plant my ass."

At this point we had another grudging silence. I stared off to my left and he scrutinized the floor.

"Whatever. You can't move in to Arlene and that's that," he said, breaking the silence.

"All right."

"What do you mean?"

"I mean *all right*. I mean *okay, fine*."

"That's *it*?" he asked. "'All *right*'? And that's it?"

"What do you want me to do? Throw a fit? I happen to understand you not wanting to live with me."

He sighed as though I had landed another catastrophe on his lap and there was just no hope.

"Why are you so eager to get me back home anyway?" I said, lighting up the next cigarette.

"You'd rather camp out in front of the library with the homeless population?" he asked.

"Of course."

"Look, the fact of the matter is you're a chronic, stubborn pain in the ass. Of course you're going to do the exact opposite of what I tell you and probably end up like a bad documentary on homeless, pregnant teens."

I could think of only one retort:

"What do *you* care?"

We had both made excellent points.

"If you moved into the camper, you'd drive me insane. You'd drive us both insane."

"Hell, I know."

Another pause.

"We weren't meant to live together, Hester. We were made to stay as far away from each other as geography allows."

"We'd be defying the devil if we tried it."

"Yeah."

"Plus, we'd have to leave town," I said.

He looked confused—all his thoughts ground to a screeching halt. "Leave town?"

"Well, I can't stay here. If I stayed in town, I'd run into my family and that would ruin my whole mysterious disappearance."

I put out cigarette number three. Fenton followed the movement of my hand and watched closely as I folded my hands on my lap, like some Catholic schoolgirl, ready to tackle the world with a Bible and a devastating look of unconcern.

"Okay," he said. "We'll leave town."

I smiled unobtrusively at the mysteries of the universe. So Fenton Flaherty had wanted to leave town all this time and found no valid reason until now. It's strange realizing everyone is in the same boat. Noah's hell-bent Ark.

"Don't get me wrong," he said, "I wouldn't want you to move in with me—ever. Under *no* circumstance. I mean, that's probably one of *the* most terrifying thoughts I can muster up. I'm just doing this for the book."

"Yeah."

"If I wasn't writing this project I would never even consider all this for a slice of a second."

"I got it, Fenton. I got it."

That night the three of us left our hometown to its own resources. It was too dark for any proper farewells; it was clear to us that we would never return there and the situation definitely required some solemn moments of sentimentality, but as I said, it was too dark. One minute we were driving past the Laundromat and the next, our only companion was the empty countryside and its trees lost in the blackness of the night. Everything went so fast. I turned around on my seat and stared at the highway trailing out behind us.

"What happened to the city limits?" I said. "I didn't even get a chance to look back at it and throw off some profound, time-defying comment."

"I hope you didn't just say that," Fenton muttered.

I *had* said that actually. What I *hadn't* bothered mentioning to Fenton was that my ten-year-old adopted son was hiding out in the back of his camper, behind the foldout bed, reading comic books. I hadn't fully worked that part out yet. In fact, I hadn't worked it out at all. But I wasn't worrying about it just then. I'd worry about it tomorrow—maybe. Or whenever it became absolutely necessary to worry about it.

Right then, I just wanted free range to wallow in the intense weirdity of the moment. A few months ago I didn't even know Philosophy Man had a camper, and now I was sitting next to him, my husband, going out into the country with my round, little cousin hiding out in the back. A few hours ago, I was standing in our living room, floundering through explanations of why I was a black sheep, sweat dripping down the sides of my face; now all needs to explain were nowhere to be found.

I never knew it was possible to feel so light.

THE CHURCH OF THE
GRAPES OF WRATH

WHEN I woke up, I was lying awkwardly against the passenger-seat door, one leg dangling on the floor, the other stretched across the seat, resting on Fenton's lap. My neck felt broken. It was still dark out, but the first gray streaks of the new day were subtly beginning to show themselves in the east. I continued to lay there unaltered. I guess there was something comforting and strange about watching Fenton's face when he didn't know that he was under surveillance. Not that it was particularly pleasant, but all the thoughts and calculations that constipated his features and loaded them up every day seemed to have drained from his skin. Maybe it was the nighttime driving—maybe this was the way he made love to Arlene. I stared more carefully with a fleeting pang of jealousy. He looked almost healthy.

Even if I actually cared about Fenton being with another woman, the sheer banality of such a boring issue as adultery would probably fail to inspire jealousy in me. But, you see, if a *car* had the power to make Fenton Flaherty a decent human being, *that* was a reason for jealousy. At least for a second. All in all, life was too good that morning for jealousy to play a lead role.

Slowly the countryside traveled into daylight, and everything seemed so mild and pretty that it was hard to believe the circumstances that had landed us there. It made me forget how absurd our histories were, the reasons that our marriage had come about, my family, and the shapeless future we now undertook to tackle. As a matter of fact, it almost made me forget the kid in the back of the camper. I never liked the sun, but this morning it seemed to hint at those untouchable legends: love and happiness.

"Life sure is good-looking from this angle," I said with the sleep still in my voice.

Fenton looked over at me in surprise and then down at my foot in his lap.

"Jesus Christ, don't you have enough space over there?" he asked, flinging it off.

"Sorry. I was asleep. But in all honesty, if anyone should have noticed my foot crawling onto your lap, don't you think it would have to be *you*?"

"I was looking at the road all night."

"You don't have *nerves* in your thighs?"

"Hester, it doesn't matter. Just please keep random body parts to yourself during this trip, okay?"

"Okay, I'll keep random body parts to myself."

There's a kind of silence that comes only after an argument has turned infantile. Needless to say, Fenton and I had a lot of these silences.

He turned on the radio and we listened to the strange lyrics

that spilled from the speakers: " . . . *he got twenty years for lovin'
her from some Oklahoma governor . . .* " This got me thinking.

"Let's not waste our time arguing about trivial things anymore," I said earnestly. "From now on, if we want to argue, let's
have it be about something significant."

"What are you talking about?"

"It just seems to me that all the arguments we have to our
credit don't create so much as a ripple in our future."

"Well, maybe I don't want any ripples in my future," he said,
stubbornly refusing to see the brilliance of my point.

"Trust me, they're inevitable."

"No, they're not."

I rolled my eyes secretly. "They *are*. The way the world is
made, there'll never be a minute in which you can sit back and
be assured you know what's going to happen next. There's always
something brewing. Even right now there is."

"Hester, it's way too early for you to be talking."

Well, I thought it would have been a cute way to introduce
the Jethro situation to him, but I saw there was little point in it.
Fenton was tired from driving through the night and strangely
wound up from the large amounts of coffee he had taken in. I
noticed his eyes were kind of bloodshot, and his thin hands had
an occasional twitch to them as they lay resting on the steering
wheel. The more I thought about it, the more I realized this was
not the time to bring up Jethro. In fact, it might have actually
been a health hazard.

I squirmed in my seat for a few seconds, determined to be
good and leave my husband in peace. Of course, that didn't work
out as planned. There was too much action in the humble do-
main that was my head.

"Fenton, I was thinking we should go to California. You know, like all the farmers in the dust-bowl era. We could re-create that whole historical route. Don't you think that in a way we're just like the people back then in their Model T Fords with their whole entourage in the back?"

Fenton's answer was sharp and instantaneous. "*No.*"

"Think about it. We're refugees just like they were. We're leaving behind everything that's familiar to us, because we know that if we would have stayed at home our lives would have been cremated by fate."

He shook his head mournfully. "The things that come out of your mouth really deserve their own soap opera."

Fenton had bizarre ways of making you want to blush at your words.

"Sorry about that," I said, smiling subtly. "So what do you think?"

"About what?"

"About California."

"Goddammit, we're not going to California. We're going to Chicago."

"Why?"

"Why? Because I'm writing a book here and not re-creating the largest historical Model T Ford migration in this country!"

"Well, what's so special about Chicago?"

"Who said there was anything special about Chicago?"

"Nobody."

"So what's your point?" he demanded nervously.

He had a tendency to freak out when the point to a discussion didn't light up in bright neon letters within three sentences.

I answered mildly. "Nothing. I'm only wondering what makes

you so gung-ho about the capital of the Midwest if there's nothing special about it."

"Oh, like going to California has some special point to it?"

"Well, the point in *that* would obviously be to see and feel the countryside the way that dust-bowl farmers did in the thirties."

"That's supposed to be a *point*?" he replied. "Why didn't you tell me *before* we got married that your Bible is *The Grapes of Wrath*?"

"Didn't occur to me," I answered.

It didn't occur to me mainly because *The Grapes of Wrath* wasn't actually my Bible; but it was a neat idea to be part of the Church of the Grapes of Wrath, and so I never bothered to set him straight on that point.

"Well, whatever," Fenton said, gripping the steering wheel harder with determination. "The reason we're going to Chicago happens to be because the conclusion to my novel takes place there. And frankly, you have no right to feel anything about it. This camper is mine, I paid for the fuel, and I have a feeling I'll be paying for the rest of the trip as well."

"Calm down. I have some cash, plus my ATM card."

He was slightly thrown off. I could tell he had counted on being the martyred supporter of his wife. But he answered with a shrug. "So we have a few more dollars. It's still my camper."

"Yeah, it is," I said, "but you're wrong about 'a few more dollars.' This is my college money we're talking about. There's enough in that account to make a brain surgeon out of me. I never understood why my parents trusted me with an ATM card for it."

"You're willing to give up brain surgery for this?"

"Yeah."

"I'm impressed."

"Well, I wasn't going to jump on a camper with a white-trash poet and not bring any money."

He was silent. Just like he had given me a church to belong to, I had just given him an adjective to his occupation; and just like it satisfied me to be a member of the dust-bowl congregation, it pleased him somewhat to be called a white-trash poet. Peace in whatever form had been restored for the time being. The sun was turning golden and the sky cloudless, the radio spurted out an old-fashioned Mexican ballad, and it seemed that to be on the road really was as tranquil and liberating as they made it out to be in books and movies. I crossed my legs and rested them on the glove compartment while Fenton maneuvered Arlene around a couple of slow trucks. I realized that this was one of those moments that ought to be left alone to ferment. It was so perfect in its constitution that to add or take anything away from it would upset the unique balance offered up by fate. The melancholy of the music, the sunlight, the benevolent way our conversation had ended. Anyone with enough sense wouldn't have touched this moment for anything in the world. Unfortunately when I have something on my mind it doesn't stay there long.

"Fenton?"

"*Please*"—he held up his hand—"only say it if it's really necessary."

"Okay."

Then I continued. "I was wondering: How do you feel about kids?"

Dark, silent annoyance. He answered in the tone of voice one uses to address a dog who just humped a chair in front of visitors—calm and morally condescending.

"Hester—please explain to me how that is 'necessary'?"

"Trust me. It's important for me to know how you feel about kids."

Fenton squirmed in his seat and then gave me a quick glance of defeat. "Well, if I answer your question, you have to promise me that you'll shut up for an entire hour—that means no reading billboards out loud or asking me whether I've had my appendix removed or what my opinion about whale hunting is—nothing. Not one sound for a whole hour. Got it?"

I waved him off. "Yeah, yeah. Just answer the question, you anal freak."

He took a troubled breath and drove his hand over his forehead like he had to recite the Bible backward or establish an alibi for a murder he committed.

"No, I don't want to have kids. And *no,* I'm not going to become soft and sentimental when I'm in my late thirties and suddenly 'fall in love' and want to procreate, littering the planet with more human life to take up what little oxygen we have left. It's just going to be me and Arlene. No kids. No wife. No nothing."

"Well, I'm with you on the oxygen part and all. But what about adoption? Like, suppose you just adopted a ten-year-old. You wouldn't be adding another human life to the world to take up any natural resources, and you wouldn't even have to deal with all the trouble of infancy. It's an instant kid. Think of it. "

He looked over at me like I was weird. "*No.* I don't want any instant, ten-year-old kids. I don't want *any* kids for chrissakes. Are you going to be able to live with that?"

"Sure."

The question really was: was *Fenton* going to be able to live with that?

Well, there's no use denying that I was somewhat dejected. I bit my lip and wondered why he seemed so religiously against the idea. It's not like I was asking him to adopt an atomic bomb. What was the big deal? Besides, for all *he* knew, this was purely hypothetical—he had absolutely no solid reason to react like this, not *yet*, at least.

I looked up at him lazily. "By the way, you're married already, so I don't see why you bother making such vigorous plans *not* to marry."

"*Hey*," he said, pointing a long finger into my face, "your hour has started."

I used my hour to think things over. The discovery was inevitable—it was never meant to be otherwise. Sometime soon, upon opening the back of the camper, Fenton was going to set eyes on Jethro. It was going to be a mess any way you looked at it—and most likely it would be one *hell* of a mess, judging by Mr. Flaherty's views on child adoption. This much I knew. And there being no way around it, was there any sense in worrying? I turned to look at Fenton. He held up his finger toward me in a stern reminder that we still had a long time to go before the end of an hour. So I leaned back in the seat again and passed the time by counting the roadkill we passed. It was better than thinking of anything that mattered.

When we stopped for lunch I ordered an extra meal under the pretense of it being "that time of the month." Fenton rolled his eyes. That is how I fed Jethro. He was doing well enough in the back. I found him wrapped in a blanket, lying behind the bed and an ever-growing collection of space pilot drawings and comic books around him. His face was sleepy and calm when he looked up.

"How's it goin'?" I said, sitting down beside him.

"Fine," he said. "How are things up front?"

"Fine."

I watched him eat a while and then decided to fill him in on a few basics.

"Just so you know: Fenton is an asshole."

He nodded.

"But that's okay," I continued, "because he's the good kind."

"How can you be a good asshole?"

"The good assholes will let you jump aboard their campers and leave town with you. They're very pliable, you see. Don't get me wrong, they give you as much shit as anyone, but he's kind of adorable in that way. It's just going to be a whole lot trickier to spring this on him than I thought it would."

This didn't faze Jethro. He looked at me from behind his sandwich and nodded.

"I don't mean to freak you out; I'm just warning you that there might be slight turbulence ahead."

"I need some coffee."

I handed him a cup of gas station coffee that I had brought for him.

"Thanks."

"Sure."

"So you're going to tell him?"

"He'll find out sooner or later. He'll have some kind of a nervous breakdown and make a deal with me, and then we'll all travel on together like a real family—well, *better* than a real family for sure."

Jethro seemed to find this plan adequate but suggested we create a little secret room to the camper where he could live—this way Fenton wouldn't find him for a long time to come and he could remain a stowaway, which would be much better.

"Obviously that would be best," I agreed. "The only problem is that Fenton would die of a heart attack if he found out we did anything to his camper."

Jethro's eyes lit up. "Well, then we'd have the camper to ourselves!"

"Jethro, murder is a bad thing."

"I thought you said he'd have a heart attack. That wouldn't be murder."

"Well, yeah, but we'd still *feel* bad."

"Oh."

"Besides, Jethro," I added, feeling all shiny about my sudden moral standards, "it's better that he knows the truth. The sooner the better, because the three of us will be stuck together for an indefinite amount of time, and it doesn't matter how many problems we have with each other as long as we're always dead honest."

Jethro took a deep sip of coffee and shrugged his shoulders.

"Why don't you tell him right now, then?" he asked.

"Because that would be just plain stupid. We're too close to home. He might drive us back."

"Oh."

"I want to make sure we're too far from home for him to turn around before I tell him."

"When will we be far enough from home for you to tell him?" Jethro asked.

"I'd say the Mississippi state line is safe."

Fenton's voice suddenly came from the front, "You think you can get your ass back up here before the dawn of the next ice age? We need to get a move on."

I winked at Jethro and climbed back outside.

The rest of the day we stuck to the freeway and didn't stray much. We drove west through Alabama, passing trucks, tuning into whatever local radio station we could receive, and drinking a lot of hot chocolate every time we fueled up. I begged Fenton to let me drive a few hours, but he refused to let anyone without a license take over Arlene. I told him that I *had* a license but just didn't have time to bring it along. He said that was the same thing. I said it wasn't the same thing by far. This got us going on an argument that lasted more than three hours and ended up being about Greenpeace. That's when I realized a large sign welcoming us to Mississippi. I sat up tensely.

THE ART OF SPILLING GUTS

THE MONSTROUS task of coming clean about the kid in the back of the camper seemed extremely impossible. I just didn't think the right words to explain this existed in the English language. I turned toward Fenton hesitantly, and the expression on my face must have been full of what was about to come because Fenton glanced nervously at me and asked me what my problem was.

"Well . . ."

My voice evaporated and I couldn't strike on a word for the life of me.

"Well—what? What?"

"Hold on! I have to make sure I'm going to formulate this properly."

He turned back toward the road, and the silence that followed was unbearable. I knew I was holding a match to a box of explosives, and there was really no graceful way of lighting the damn thing. You could formulate it any old way you wanted, in the end there would always be little Jethro, ten years old, sitting wrapped in a blanket in the back of the camper.

"Okay, listen," I began suddenly, "remember when you went to climb mountains in Switzerland?"

"It was for a piece I was writing," he answered impatiently. "I didn't go to Switzerland to play fucking Heidi. I was writing a poem."

This threw me off somewhat and I started up again all rusty.

"So when you were hiking in Switzerland—or rather, when you were in Switzerland gathering material for whatever, the poem or whatever—"

"Hester, for the love of God—get to the point!"

"I was only trying to butter it up for your delicate digestive system! But if you think you can take it raw, I'll slap it on your plate with the blood running over the edge of it."

"The *point*, Hester."

"The point is that my cousin Jethro is in the back of your camper right now. He's ten years old, and we became real good friends while you were in Switzerland."

"Excuse me?" he said.

"I said there's a kid in the back of your camper."

Hesitation.

"Figuratively or—literally?"

I was a little confused at how I could mean that figuratively.

"Literally," I told him.

"In the back of Arlene?"

I looked at him earnestly. "Fenton, you're not making this any easier."

He said nothing. His upper lip went through a curious quivering motion, though, and his hands began to nervously fondle the wheel. I just stared in fascination, waiting as patiently as I could for the show to commence. After a minute or so his eyes darted at the rearview mirror. He stepped on the brake and frantically swung the wheel to the left, bringing Arlene to a breathless halt in the strip of grass that divided the freeway. The door swung open and he disappeared to the back. I lost no time and tumbled out into the cold after him.

The back door was open by the time I got there, and I found Fenton already inside. This would be interesting. Rubbing my hands together, I took the liberty of preparing a haphazard explanation. I also made a mental note to prepare a monologue the next time I decided to have a hand at chaos. It was one thing to turn the world upside down with a jolly work ethic, but one *has* to label these things—otherwise you can find yourself out on a highway divider, trying to find one trace of logic to point out.

Well, I soon realized there were no logistics involved. One doesn't map out emotions with a flow diagram. I was crazy about Jethro. I had to leave town. He asked to come along and I said all right. That was all there was to it.

Just as I was about to mount the steps, Fenton reappeared. He shut the door behind him and our eyes locked for a matter of seconds. He was a mess of coffee and sleep deprivation, but other than that he looked relatively calm. I was surprised. There were no obvious signs of mental damage.

"Fenton, I realize you weren't expecting to find a small kid in the back of the camper today. Or any day really."

He brushed past me and I continued.

"And because I openly admit to no reasonable justification, it's fine if you wanna throw a fit. Really. Whatever makes this easier on you."

I had followed him around the driver's door. He got in without a word and slammed the door shut in my face. I didn't think anything of it until, of course, the engine started up and the camper jolted into motion. I watched the camper take off into the distance. It felt like my stomach suddenly gave way and was dropping indefinitely into a black distance. Well, I had every right to be unnerved—after all, this was my very first time being abandoned on the side of a freeway.

There's relatively little you can do in such a situation, by the way. You can flag down a car of course, but after so many movies of hitchhiking mishaps, most people don't feel very gung-ho about sticking their thumbs out over a freeway. There are other things you can do—call someone or knock on a door, but you'd need a phone or a door for this, of which I had neither. In all honesty, the cold became so persistent that there wasn't much else for me to do but be pissed at Fenton. Here he pretended like he could take it all like it is, but when it came down to the potency of undiluted truth, the first thing he does is act like a freshly baptized fool. What's he going to do? Go cross-country alone with the kid? Ha! I decided to let him try it. Not that I had much choice in the matter.

It was getting to be dark by that time. The icy wind blew the hair over my face. I wrapped the scarf around my neck and head as many times as I could and planted my hands underneath my armpits. Then, realizing that I had three loose cigarettes and a lighter in my dress pocket, I lost no time and supplied myself with the only pleasure left to me.

It didn't take long for a car to slow down. I watched it roll up to me. It was nice that some part of humanity was taking an interest in me, but on the other hand all of F's stories about murder, rape, and kidnappings for government-sponsored mind experiments rushed back to me all at once. He told me all about what he called the milk-bottle people, meaning the missing people whose black-and-white faces stare over your breakfast table when you eat cereal. But I was never one to be scared of dark alleyways or bums coming up to you in the yellow light of late-night bus rides.

"You all right there?" a voice came from the car.

It was a guy in his thirties with one of those thick mustaches that went out of fashion with the gold rush. He wore a baseball cap that said "Beer" on it. He didn't look much like a government agent. I decided it was safe to enter into a conversation with him.

"I'm freezing my ass off," I said.

"You need a ride somewhere?"

"No."

"What are you doing out here on the highway?"

"Long story. My husband will be back soon enough, though."

"Well, get in the car."

"You're gonna wait here for my husband to get back?"

"Yeah."

I shrugged my shoulders and got in on the passenger side. I knew it was probably not the greatest thing to do, getting into a stranger's car and all, but I can safely say that at this point I would have gotten into a car with the devil, or any other cast member of the Bible. The cold is extremely persuasive that way.

"Well, thanks," I said, slamming the door shut.

I got comfortable in front of the heater while I looked him over. He wore a T-shirt that said "Can your beer do this?" And then there was a picture of a well-endowed white-trash lady on the verge of taking off her tank top.

I smiled. "You mind if I give you an honest opinion on your attire?"

"No."

"Well, I think the theme is slightly overstated."

"What do you mean?"

"Well, you got 'beer' written on your cap *and* on your T-shirt. It would look a lot classier if you only wore one article of clothing with 'beer' on it."

"You think?"

"Yeah. I mean, I'm the last person you'd wanna go to for fashion advice, but purely from a literary standpoint, if you had the word 'beer' written on you only *once,* the effect would be much more powerful."

He looked a little abashed. "God, I don't think I ever looked at it that way. My brother gave me the T-shirt—I wouldn't have bought it myself."

"Don't worry about it. As I said, it's purely an editorial point I'm making here. If you're going to talk about actual *clothes* I'm not any better."

And I wasn't. I was wearing a long-sleeved bright red dress with a tear on the left hip that I had fixed with a blue scrap of cloth a few months earlier. My socks were thick, long, and striped. And my scarf was bright green.

"The way I see it, it's the really badly dressed people that lead meaningful lives," I said. I didn't really believe this, of course. But it sure made for a cute phrase to throw out.

Then, realizing I had a cigarette in my hand, I asked him if he minded me smoking in his car.

"Go right ahead," he said, pulling out a little compartment that turned out to be an ashtray. "I don't mind, just as long as you know what it does to you."

"Oh, I never cared much about my health."

"You only got one body. You might as well look after it," he answered.

I was surprised. He made an obnoxious fact come across real well and easy. It must have been the first time that I realized you could point out someone's faults right to their face and just be as easy about it as though you're telling him there's a hair in his soup. I was delighted. The way my mother always went about these things, it was like watching someone fight with constipation. Just the way she began with my name made me cringe.

"I'm Hester, by the way," I said, depositing the cigarette in my mouth and reaching my hand over.

"Dan—short for Daniel," he answered, shaking it. And then he asked, "Where'd your husband drive off to? You realize there are people who'd take advantage of a girl standing around here by the highway like this."

"So they say."

"Well, it's true. No man in his right mind would leave his wife alone by a highway at night."

"Dan, my husband isn't even three hundred *miles* in the vicinity of his 'right mind.'"

"Why did you marry him, then?" he asked.

"Because I'm worse than he is—by quite a bit."

I was in no mood to go over the Jethro situation or point out the specifics of our marriage or narrate any other part of my life for that matter—I was bored sick of my existence, and so I turned the tables.

"What about you? Are you married?"

Dan looked sternly moral as he answered, like he had his hand on a Bible. "Yes, ma'am. Five years now. Best thing I ever did was get married to that woman."

It was a beautifully executed statement and left me with nothing to say. I shivered.

He went on, "I didn't have great expectations. I mean, look at me. I just thought I'd take whatever comes along, you know? I thought I'd be lucky if I got so much as a raccoon interested in me."

I smiled. "Well, you know, in some cases I'm sure a raccoon is a better choice."

"Maybe so, but I don't know of any raccoon that could keep up with the girl I finally found. I met her at the Chicken Fest—you know, the one in Kentucky. I just couldn't help staring at her—at that yellow dress flying all around her knees in the breeze. I wasn't looking in a pervert kind of way or anything, of course."

"Of course."

"I knew I was looking at the girl I already loved. I also knew it was bad manners to stare, but it was like it is with gold—you can't tear your eyeballs off it."

"I've never seen a real good chunk of gold," I said.

"Well, the lady I'm married to is made out of something like it. Except that you can find gold mostly anywhere in this world. You can't find her anywhere other than with me. She came over to me that day at the Chicken Fest and started talking just as easy as anything. We talked about fruit drinks for an awful long time . . ."

The fondness of the moment was reflected in his voice, which became slow and soft, tangled up in memories, but his eyes remained wide open when he talked and his mouth never once cracked into a smile.

"Well," he said, "next thing I know we're married. I couldn't say exactly how it happened, and I wouldn't want to think about it either. It happened, and that's all that matters. I try not to think about what she could see in a guy like me. I'm superstitious that way. I think it'll make her take a closer look and realize she's made some kind of mistake."

Those awkward words put together so imperfectly smashed to bits everything I had ever hoped for—or felt I ever could hope for. It disturbed me, being that I could not remember ever having been susceptible to corny-ass romance stories. I was caught off guard. I felt emptied out of all current issues—everything that seemed to have always been on my mind was drained away. I felt vanquished.

"That's a picture of her right there," he said, pointing to a Polaroid taped to the rearview mirror.

He turned on the light for me as I leaned over to examine the picture of a woman grinning shyly, with a cone-shaped party hat strapped to her head. The way her lips curved uncertainly up at the corners made her look like a small-town librarian who had struck it rich by accidentally having collided with the man of her dreams. Her face was red, maybe from laughter or maybe from a cheap heating system. She wore a plaid skirt and an unflattering brown turtleneck sweater that stuck to her tightly and exposed a waist that bore similarities to a lifesaver. Her hair was styled by a beauty parlor and it looked terrible and sweet the way it was almost glued into place under that miserable party hat.

So this lady slightly bulging from her knitwear was the blinding beauty that made him disbelieve his luck? I felt a little speechless.

I mean, people didn't really love each other. At least not harmlessly. Maybe there were couples out there who were in love with each other *passionately,* like Romeo and Juliet, ready to jump from cliffs and dig toothpicks into their eyeballs to prove their love. And maybe there were people out there who loved with more force than a nuclear power plant. I've known people like that, and every time they opened their mouths I wondered how they'd managed to stay alive this long. Shouldn't they have exploded from sheer emotional overload long ago? I never heard of so much stress.

I knew there were people out there who claimed to be in love. But it caught me off guard to think that there were real people out there—people who went to Chicken Fests to fall in love, and not only did they find love there, but they managed to find the real live version of "true love," the kind that's a myth. And that's why they got married, and that's how they lived: effortlessly, easily, and also happily, just as though they didn't know any better. Like they grew up so far from civilization that they didn't know it wasn't human not to be complex. My mind took off like a gospel choir going full speed ahead.

Just then my door was ripped open and a gust of ice blew my scarf into Dan's face. Turning, I found Fenton standing there with his features almost entirely hidden by some kind of knit hat that looked like he had stolen it from a German dwarf. Only a few bright hairs stuck forth and danced in the wind.

"What are you doing?" he asked, his calm voice coming muffled from a scarf.

Reality brought back with it my slow smile.

"Talking with Dan."

Fenton peered over at Dan.

"Hi there," Dan said.

"Hey," Fenton replied.

"This is my husband," I explained to Dan.

He nodded.

"Well, we better go—we're letting all the cold air in," I said when it looked like the conversation wasn't going to bloom into a heated debate on world peace.

Dan looked at me like a saint in a religious painting. "You take care, Hester."

"You too, Dan."

And that was how Fenton found out about Jethro hiding in the back of his camper. That was how the acid February wind tore through my clothes by the side of the highway, and that's how the innocent ramblings of some guy with a pickup truck emptied me out and made my eyes water.

Walking back to the camper, I threw a glance over my shoulder at the pickup truck getting back on the road. The emotions Dan had ignited shot through me once more. Then they vanished, and for the time being sentimentality once again became a lost art.

As I climbed back into the camper Fenton was already seated in the driver's seat, ready to pull away, and to my surprise, Jethro sat beside him. He looked healthy, sitting there with his supply of comic books on his lap, and smiling at me like a face on an oatmeal box. I slid up next to him on the seat and patted him on the head.

It seemed that neither Fenton nor I felt any desire to start in on an argument about the kid sitting between us. In fact, we wrapped the whole ordeal up in a few words.

"Next time you plan to be a hippie and add some more kids to your rainbow tribe, let me know before you hide any of them in my camper," he said.

"Sure. And next time you decide to leave me stranded somewhere where the temperature is below freezing point, make sure I'm not just wearing a flannel."

"All right."

I had never been more in love with Fenton than I was at that moment, as he steered Arlene back onto the freeway and the uneven grass made us sway like passengers on a boat. I'm not saying that I actually *was* in love with him, but rather that usually I was a lot less in love with him. I had always had a strong suspicion that most of Fenton's life was the way it was only because he liked a good old-fashioned play.

We took Jethro into a little thrift store in Clarksdale after that. Now that he was officially a human entity in the camper, I thought it was high time he had a change of clothes. The thing was, Jethro's idea of packing had been to bring his entire comic book collection and about three pairs of underwear. Both his little suitcase *and* the plastic bag that he brought were filled with nothing else.

The store was called Clothes Make the Man and was on the verge of shutting down for the night when we slid in. It was one of those places where no matter how hard you try, you can't find anything that you'd actually wear in public unless someone paid you a lot of money for it, but Jethro seemed not to mind. In fact, he started enthusiastically pulling out clothes and tossing them on the little pile we had started for him. That kid had strange tastes. Even Fenton couldn't help being a little baffled.

"You sure you wanna get this one with all the reindeer on it?" he asked.

"Yeah!"

"Oh, all the Christmas clothes are half off, by the way," the old lady behind the counter offered up.

Not that we needed that encouragement.

We drove much farther that night. It felt good having everything laid out on the table like that.

DON'T MY GAL LOOK FINE

NEXT MORNING the sunlight spilled in through the greasy camper windows and trailed across the laundry scattered on the floor and over my cheek. My body was cold underneath the odds and ends that Fenton called blankets, and although he was lying next to me on the narrow camper bed, we couldn't move close to each other to preserve heat—it made him feel claustrophobic. Generally we spent all those nights pressed to opposite sides of the bed, and between fighting for blankets and trying to keep *on* the bed, one didn't get much of that bottomless sleep. Nevertheless, that morning I woke up feeling like some doctor had administered the right kind of medicine.

Jethro was spread out in a sleeping bag on the floor with Walter, his toy giraffe, sprawled over his face. I reached over and pulled the giraffe off his face by the rice in its butt. Then I turned onto my back and stared at the ceiling where Fenton had scrawled in black paint: "*Once a year my dad feels the need to set fire to the house—either that or burn down the yard.*"

I was trying to figure out if that meant something deeply baffling or if he was just being a pretentious idiot. In any case, I loved finding odd bits of Fenton's scrawled thoughts, partly because he was so possessive of them; but mainly I liked it because he strictly forbade me to read stuff I found lying around.

The watch he had taped onto the kitchen cabinet said it was 7:15 a.m. It was Sunday. I got out of bed, put on my coat, and made my way to the door. There was no need to get dressed, because in this temperature there was really no need to get *un*-dressed. I pushed my weight hard against the door and turned the handle.

The outside world seemed to reflect the peace of the camper's lifeless interior. We were in Kentucky. We had gotten lost the night before and drifted far off the freeway, over small roads that turned into even smaller roads. The frustration of late-night driving and being helplessly embedded in the middle of nowhere had left Fenton inconsolable. After stringing a bunch of unlikely swear words together in one impressive sausage that made Je-thro burst into a wide-eyed grin, he turned Arlene off the road and slammed on the brakes. We all went to bed with the camper parked exactly there.

In the daylight I realized just how awkward the angle of the camper was. We were facing a solitary tree and the back door hov-ered slightly over the edge of the road's gray concrete. I jumped to the ground and got my first impression of Kentucky as a beau-tifully haunted playground. The grass was pale green and yellow with remnants of snow still visible. The trees were sparse and bare. In the distance I could spot two whitewashed farmhouses. Other than that there was nothing. All those drawling bluegrass wails now made perfect sense.

Well, I put a cigarette in my mouth and spent an uncommonly

long time setting light to it. After inhaling deeply, my eyelids fell shut and I enjoyed the subtle drugging of my respiratory system in peace and quiet. I do believe that drag out there in the Kentucky hills could have been a monstrosity in the department of miracle moments; but then Dan's remark came at me out of nowhere—the one about only having one body. And that was the end of it. He was right. I had a chronic cough all my life; why was I sucking smoke into the lungs? It's strange suddenly caring about your health when you've never spent a second thinking about it before. It was kind of disturbing to become so goddamn righteous to tell you the truth. But when your conscience barges in uninvited, there's no hope left for filthy habits. I decided I'd quit smoking. After that cigarette of course.

As my last cigarette burned between my mittens, I began to walk along the road, coughing and smoking. It was an eerie Sunday morning. There was religion in the air and last night's wind was still sweeping over the desolate road, tugging at the grass and bending the stubborn branches of trees. I passed a red barn that stood across the street, burned against a milky sky. The sun had been swallowed up long ago, leaving everything in a dampened glow that added strange sentiments to this Jesus Hallelujah break of day. I could almost feel some sinner crying in an ecstatic breakthrough—kneeling on the floorboards of a country church because the roof was being torn apart and some kind of divine flush of light was drowning him. The panorama was dead and silent, but just walking down that road I understood there was more going on there than in any nightclub or on any TV channel.

My thoughts traveled down strange corridors. I'd never felt at home until the moment I actually left home behind many state lines. To think that this day would pass and crumble to pieces and during the whole ordeal of it I wouldn't once have to deal with any of the obnoxious flavors that made up home—no mother commenting on the color coordination of my clothes, no father getting drunk on muscle-formula protein drinks, no sister dragging her painful existence across my path. Lord knows I'd like to tell you just how it felt walking in Kentucky with those thoughts, but nobody ever bothered coining the necessary words.

A million doctors will label me a victim of traumatic childhood experiences because I say this. Only, I don't consider my past traumatic in any sense and I should know best. The past is the past and it was only made to be left behind. That's where it was as I took that walk, and I touched on it only like I would turn over a dead raccoon with the tip of my shoe, to see what made it die.

I walked until my body warmed up and the wind and blood circulation burned my face. My last cigarette had come to an end. I bid farewell to it, standing in front of a small gas station that had materialized around a bend in the road. The place didn't exactly look like it was beating Burger King in gross income, but still, it had that patient confidence about it that indicated it would probably sit there selling fuel far longer than any Burger King would be poisoning human bodies. It had that eerie sense of endurance that only dilapidated businesses seem to have. It was closed, and I was about to turn back when I noticed someone sitting on the floor.

"Hello," I said, walking over.

The stranger looked up, momentarily confused. Maybe he thought the human race had died out.

"Hi," he replied a little awkwardly. "How's it going?"

"Good enough for me. How's it going for you?"

"My car ran out of gas. I'm just waiting for this place to open."

"That sucks."

We looked each other over just as calmly as though we were scanning a shelf for the right brand of soup. We were both a little too wrapped up in coats, scarves, and hats to make out anything significant, but I noticed the man wore an old porkpie hat and wrapped around it was a thick woolen scarf with a repetitive Winnie-the-Pooh pattern. His face was unshaven and his cheeks were flushed bright, like he was a little kid that had accidentally grown into a man. It was the first time I saw someone with cheeks like my own, and immediately I nurtured ideas of having found a secret twin brother.

"I like your scarf," I said.

"Oh, I like your scarf too."

"Why, thanks."

I had never flirted with someone until that morning. It was in my nature to call people "honey" sometimes but that's just good manners. Not even with Fenton—*especially* not with Fenton. I had only ever flirted with my husband like a bored kid flirts with sex, drugs, and rock 'n' roll. I had never felt the need to become sweet and vulnerable, you understand. But that morning my smile crawled along just a little slower than it usually did, and I'll be damned if you couldn't have tasted sugar on my lips.

"You're on a family vacation or something?" he asked, seeing a bit of the camper in the distance.

"Hell, no."

He was expecting more than just that, but I wasn't about to let it out that easily.

"Well, this isn't the time of the year for road trips," he said.

"We're not on a road trip. That's our home. We live in that thing."

"Who's 'we'?"

"Me and Jethro and Fenton," I answered slyly. I was acting like I had magnificent secrets to harbor. And maybe I did. In any case, I didn't want to let it slip that I was married.

The way he said "Ah," with a slow nod, made me think somehow I had given it up anyway.

"Are you from this part of the country?" I asked.

He sighed with a crooked grin and shook his head. "No, unfortunately I'm from Florida."

I nodded slowly but didn't let on that I was a native Floridian. Coincidence was getting dangerously eerie and probably the best thing to do was ignore it.

"I'm driving a prosthetic leg to my grandpa in Kansas," he continued suddenly. "I know it's a ridiculous thing to be doing. He won't let me mail it. Under normal circumstances I would have lied and told you I was going to a family funeral or something."

"What makes this an abnormal circumstance?"

"It must be your eyes—do you always x-ray people like that? I feel like I'm naked."

"Well, I guess that's very sweet of you to say."

"Oh, yeah, it is. It's definitely a compliment."

Another silence passed. I stood there, with my hands in my pockets, not quite knowing how to smoothly pass these voids by, now that I was a nonsmoker. Seemed that I always had an easier time passing stubborn minutes with a cigarette in my fingers. Where do you put your goddamn hands if you don't smoke?

"This scarf isn't mine, by the way," the stranger said. "I just needed something to wrap over my ears, and this was the only thing I found in the back of my car."

"Oh."

That's when the camper pulled up beside us. Jethro's head stuck out the window. Behind him Fenton's eyes gleamed critically.

"Hey!" Jethro called, waving. "Fenton says we gotta go—and he used the F word."

"There are about three million F words, Jethro," I said.

He looked daunted. "The F-U word—you know."

"You're going to have to talk in real words with me, honey. We're not in your mom's living room. No one's going to flinch."

"The fuck word."

"Ah."

Fenton leaned over toward Jethro. "Are we done with the English lesson? Can we get a move on, please?"

I turned back to the stranger, who had already gotten to his feet and was holding out his hand to me. We shook hands and agreed it was good to have met.

I jumped over a cold puddle and climbed aboard the camper, feeling like my insides suddenly had central heating. Both Fenton and Jethro stared at me as I settled into my seat. I looked back at them as unaffectedly and blankly as I could, but that kind of stuff is never easy with my complexion. I was burning bright.

"Mornin'," I told them.

"Mornin'," Jethro answered.

Fenton didn't say anything. He just pushed the camper into first gear and steered us back onto the road. There went my first romance, leaving me with nothing to console me but the skeletons of trees floating by.

"Who the hell was that?"

I turned to Fenton, surprised that he was interested.

"Just somebody driving a prosthetic leg to his grandpa."

"What's a prosthetic leg?" Jethro asked.

"A fake leg, honey."

"Well, I gotta tell you, Hester," Fenton began again, out of no-where, "it's embarrassing the way you throw yourself at random guys."

I looked at him kind of strange. "Okay, Dad."

"I'm serious," he said. "It's really kind of vulgar."

I laughed.

"I'm not joking."

"I know—that's why I'm laughing."

"You just performed such a tasteless cliché—the whole crush-on-a-mysterious-stranger bullshit. It's so vulgar and stupid."

"Speaking of tasteless clichés, I know of a certain somebody who went hiking in Switzerland and did more than just ask the milkmaids for directions to the next ski lodge."

He sighed. "I wish you'd stop bringing that up every two minutes. There's no need to get all weird. I'm just saying it's not attractive when a woman fucking rubs herself up against every hobo she meets on a road trip."

"You're right, maybe I should take a pregnancy test."

"She wasn't rubbing against him," Jethro mentioned offhand-edly. He never seemed to be paying attention, but he always was.

"Obviously I don't have to mean that *literally*, Jethro," he snapped. "The point is I could read what was going on in her head from ten miles away, and it wasn't exactly something you'd publish in a storybook for kids."

Jethro looked confused. "What was she thinking about?"

"Nothing. Can't you just read a comic book or draw another alien or something?"

"They're not aliens. They're humans. They're just wearing space helmets."

"Well, I never saw a space helmet shaped like an amoeba," Fenton mumbled under his breath.

"They're spacemen from the *future*."

"Oh, of course," he chuckled coldly. "You know, you can't use that excuse every time you realize your space helmets or your oxygen masks have fatal flaws. Real life doesn't work like that, Jethro. If I wrote something that looked like your space helmet there, and nobody understood it—do you think I could tell a publisher, 'Hey, man, this is literature from the future'? I highly doubt it."

"You don't get it," Jethro complained. "The helmet is curved like that because it gives the pilot double vision."

Fenton tore his eyes off the road and blinked at the drawing that was taped to the rearview mirror and dangled beautifully right in the center of Arlene's cockpit.

"And that part right there?" he asked. "Is his ass deformed or does that protrusion also serve some technical purpose?"

Jethro narrowed his eyes at the spaceman's rear end for a moment. He seemed to turn the lump in that gentleman's anatomy over in his head for a matter of seconds. Then he said, "That's spaceman George. See, actually there's nothing wrong with his— ass"—he uttered the word carefully—"but the whole drawing is like how the other guy sees it. The other guy's called spaceman Jimmy. So that's just how Jimmy sees everything, because there's this poisonous gas in the air that distorts normal dimensions."

Fenton smiled. "Well, doesn't everything just conveniently fall into place?"

"Yeah. They're actually kind of like cowboys—except in outer space," Jethro added, oblivious to all sarcasm.

This conversation trickled along pleasantly for another hour or so, and I leaned back, glad to be left entirely out of it. It was a beauty of a dialogue, I might add. Fenton and Jethro could really outdo just about anyone when it came to the art of tearing apart subject matter. The conversation ran like water over pebbles— from ray-guns to time machines to things I didn't even know the meaning of. Fenton was pointing out the technicalities of how impossible everything was with fervor and the usual broom up his ass, and Jethro solved the said problems without so much as a flinch. Any adult would have given up long ago; it took someone as truly anal as Fenton to carry such subject matters through to a child's contentment.

This was the life. This was the midday high.

In fact, it looked like the three of us might have fallen into regularity. Maybe this was *not* a freak accident after all. Maybe we were supposed to all end up here together, and it wasn't just my decision to leave home. Not that I'd actually believed that, but I won't lie—it was hard to cast this possibility out of my head when the afternoon was so goddamn golden.

Yep, it sure seemed like we'd successfully crossed some kind of hurdle. Of course, whenever you think you've crossed something as vague as a hurdle successfully, you know that can't possibly be true.

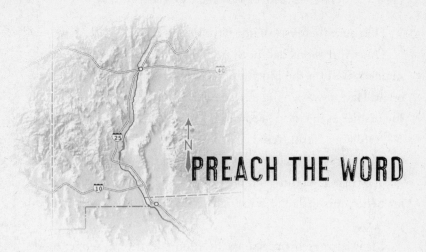

PREACH THE WORD

YOU KNOW that myth about kids always having to pee when you're on the road? Well, it's true. After a few hours of that Sunday, it seemed to me like Jethro's sole purpose on earth was to urinate. The circumstances were merciless. What with Jethro's hyperactive bladder and the camper not being equipped with a bathroom. On top of that my recent abdication from cigarettes was weighing hard on my soul and the only radio station Arlene tuned into was airing a show called "Reverend Hatton's Lost Sheep Hour." Need I say more? I might have wondered with distaste where the beautiful morning had gone, but I didn't. Something maternal in me didn't allow me to roll my eyes when Jethro announced that yet another bathroom break was in order. And I guess it was that same piece of machinery that made me say placidly, "Okay, honey."

And so Fenton and I shared another one of those uninspired moments by the roadside, watching Jethro make for the bushes.

"Just look on the bright side," I said.

"There's a bright side to this?"

"I'm sure there is. We just have to find it."

Our expressions had been numbed long ago and our eyes remained fixed on the indefinite distance. In the background Reverend Hatton was giving advice to a lady who was convinced that the cashier at the local hardware store was possessed by the devil.

"Oh, Lord," I muttered.

Jethro was still selecting what bush to make use of. He had a habit of using the most remote bush available. Contrary to popular belief, this little kid had high standards in both hygiene and privacy.

I leaned myself up against the door on the passenger's side and got out one of those books I had taken from the library, *Who's Who in Charles Dickens*. Reverend Hatton asked his caller for more details, and I began to stare at the notes I had taken down on one of the pages. *"He will hug you and kiss you and tell you more lies than leaves on the green tree or stars in the skies."*

I got most of my advice from old blues and folk songs. I didn't believe there was any sense in getting your philosophy anyplace else—not when people had sung things like " . . . *you may be a little rockin', but baby, you all right with me . . .* " Didn't that sum up just about every relationship between a woman and a man?

I swung my feet up on the seat and began to get comfortable with this new line of reasoning. I loved it when I caught hold of something that I could tear apart until the end of eternity. My mind loved to suck on ideals and impossibilities, and once I had started rolling, things didn't easily get in the way. But of course my carefree concentration was not immune to everything. I felt something against my feet, and found Fenton's ink-stained fingers trailing aimlessly over my ankles. My body became tense. This was clearly a violation of the "random body part" rule.

I looked up very slowly. Fenton smiled at me like a fox would smile in a children's book illustration. I couldn't return the favor, unfortunately. I couldn't even blink. My eyelids were frozen into the air. I stared back at him like I was staring straight into his headlights on a dark night. Our eyes were interlocked in this way for a few long seconds. It was strange in the sense that we didn't usually bother looking at each other at all. Certainly not into each other's eyes. And even if we did, it had never been without sarcasm or a sneer.

Well, I knew right there that something was wrong, but there was little time to engage in anything sensible. You don't wonder much about the seconds to come when miracles erupt before your eyes. And this wasn't one of those disputable miracles like visions of the Virgin Mary in oil spills; this was a *true* miracle—like your refrigerator talking to you one morning as you enter the kitchen, or a fork melting in your hand for no particular reason. It was the kind that defied the laws of the physical universe.

I admit I was flustered. More so than the time I had to explain to our family counselor why I masturbated. I was fourteen at the time and ready to sink into despair. But what can you do? Eventually, I just had to shrug my shoulders at the doctor and say: "'Cause it feels good, asshole. Why the hell do *you* do it?"

But that afternoon in the camper, I couldn't find anything to say at all. I dropped my eyes down again to the handwriting that traveled over all the blank, battered edges of the library book. *"Blues on my shelf . . . and there's blues on my bed 'cause I'm sleeping by myself."* My cheeks burned, swollen with all the blood that rushed through them. Sure, Fenton had sometimes cracked a grin before, just to let the world know how pathetic it was, but this smile right there was subtle, almost tired-looking. It was clean, defenseless, and seemed to have no grounding. It was bottomless. It was un-nerving. Any way you looked at it, it was the twilight zone.

I tried to ignore him. Tried to ignore the expression that ate into my face, the silence waiting to be filled by some question or insult or laugh—even the fingers and palms of his hands that crawled further up my legs. But how long could I keep that up?

"You all right?" I asked, cautiously looking up from the book.

"Yep."

His fingers crawled around the heels of my feet, and then with some kind of weird movement that belonged in an Indian pop-video routine, my legs were suddenly on either side of his hips and his grip had moved to the hollow underneath my knees. The book slipped from my grip in the process and tumbled to the floor, landing hard against the window. I was left with my empty hands outstretched on the seat, feeling awkward. I probably should have laughed. That would have been the right thing to do, considering how great that move was, but remember: I was almost paralyzed with fear at this point. The only way I could explain the situation to myself was that Fenton was dying of cancer or something and was having an emotional breakdown in true Technicolor style. And I'm not trying to be witty, I really thought that.

I propped myself up on my elbows and stared hard at his cloudless features. When we had married there were certain un-spoken rules that stood firm as the basis to our existence. We didn't like each other; we just enjoyed the fascination we were able to extract from the daily freak show of which we were both leading attractions. Unlimited free tickets were all we asked for. There wasn't any passion and there never *would* be; we were just characters from a book with a bad title—"Transplant." We weren't human—that was the great thing. We were probably the only two people on the face of the earth who gladly traded romance for neglect. As far as I was concerned, there was a lot of junk that trailed behind romance, and I wanted none of it.

And now Fenton threatened to spoil it all. His hands had come to the end of the wool stocking and were traveling over my hips, up my back, without considering any of the above facts.

"Fenton, what the hell do you think you're doing?"

In all honesty I was kind of, well, starkly impressed. My eyelids fell shut and everything just plummeted into place, like it had all been choreographed in some past lifetime in a barn. Suddenly it seemed impossible to be satisfied. Every kiss just needed to be deeper and every touch needed to leave a dent in order to be good enough. Boy, I had no idea horniness could be so classy. It was weird, folks. All careful calculations in my head evaporated.

I remember pulling away to tell him, "You know, this would be romantic if it weren't for the music."

The radio had given Reverend Hatton a rest and was blaring loud bluegrass with banjos and fiddles tearing up everything left and right. Fenton stared at me, kind of disturbed.

He pulled me back impatiently and said something like, "Jesus, Hester, how can you stop and comment on the fucking music?"

Just as we were going to take up from where we had left off, and maybe be satisfied for the first time ever, the door flew open and Jethro's round face stared blankly at us over the car seat.

Fenton got off from on top of me and slid over to the wheel, calm and expressionless. Luckily we were still dressed. I followed his example and made space for Jethro to climb in. However, the ominous silence indicated it was time for me to make an official press statement. And since I didn't want to lie, I chose to interpret freely: "We were just looking for something."

He smiled discreetly. "Did you find it?"

"Well, not exactly—no."

"You guys need some more time?"

"No, thanks, Jethro. We'll find it sooner or later."

Then we were back on the highway—quiet, a little dumb-founded, and not sure whether the smiles we wanted to give in to were kosher or not. The steady pumping of bluegrass through Arlene's speakers continued.

"I am a roving Gambler/Gambled all around!/Ever I meet with a deck of cards/I lay my money down!"

Chorus: "Lay my money down, Lay my money down!"

I joined in on the third chorus.

Boy, did we all feel weird after that. None of us said anything for about three million hours.

THEY TELL ME JORDAN IS DEEP AND WIDE

THAT NIGHT we went to bed as though our horniness had not gotten the best of us. I lay on one side of the bed and Fenton on the other. My face was turned to the back and his to the front of the camper. The gap between us was as large as it had always been, maybe even larger. Were we trying to prove something? Maybe we were trying to get back up from the pavement as though there was no blood on our knees? But how do you do that? How do you gracefully play off a slip of the tongue, a train wreck, a collision . . . how do you pretend you aren't interested? It was strange, fixating so hard on nothingness when it is such a blatant lie. How do you avoid the impertinent embarrassments of reality? How do you dismiss an incident that tackles your memory to the ground every moment of the day and leaves it a bloody pulp? How do you sit through that and smile with the nonchalance and grace of boredom?

Well, Fenton and I just closed our eyes.

I guess most girls want this every second of their lives, even when they're married and loading shopping bags into a minivan. But when you've never wanted anything in the department of burning sunset romance, it's a whole different story. It's like a horror story. You never look out for it. You never expect it. And when suddenly passion bursts from some bush like a speed cop at the side of a freeway, you might feel somewhat slaughtered. And maybe that's how it should be, but I've always made a point of avoiding all that, doing my best since third grade to abolish every opportunity that might lead to some romantic comedy in my life. The fact that one day something out of a pair of unlikely eyes would shake me up like this could of course leave me no other way but stranded with little of my small sanity intact.

I don't know if things ever went back to normal. It became sort of hard to tell what was normal. Seems like no matter how soundly you make it out of the twilight zone, that place leaves you handicapped, paranoid, and with no sense of balance or direction. We did just fine by ignoring all traces of what had happened. I hardly looked at my husband at all the next day. Those cold blue eyes were emptied out of all remembrance, and although it made me feel like some kind of a lone nut, it might have been better than finding traces of something that shouldn't have happened. What happened was an accident. Who wants to come upon signs of one's personal disease in someone else's features? If you have a third eyebrow do you want every passerby's smile to remind you of it? Chances are you'd rather forget all about God's little mishaps.

So I brushed the crumbs from my lap and decided I'd never think about it again.

But I'd dreamt about it. And when I woke up the next morning, the first thing I thought of was the way in which Fenton had put his hands on my burning cheeks. So much for *that* plan.

In a way everything crumbled to pieces when I realized I was more blood and flesh than I thought. It was disturbing. Everything that I appreciated about my own life was no longer there. Assurances that I grew up with from the time I was conceived—they all drifted out of position and proportion in a single gray morning. The one thing that I knew I could always depend on was the boundless immaturity of my soul that nothing could touch. And suddenly, here I was, sitting out on the camper's steps by myself early in the morning, tapping a spatula nervously against my legs. My smile was nowhere to be found.

"What are you doing with the spatula out there?"

I turned around, and there he stood with a yawn in the doorway and his hair looking like the statue of liberty.

"I was going to make pancakes for Jethro," I said.

"With *what*?"

"I don't know. I guess it was just an idealistic maternal thought that derailed into reality."

"Well, a spatula alone isn't going to get you a pancake, and if you don't mind, I'd like my kitchen tools to stay clean," he said, grabbing the spatula from my grip and disappearing back into the black interior.

Fenton became himself again within the very second he had slid off me the day before. He became himself more so than ever, in fact. He never mentioned what had happened—neither with words, nor looks, nor smiles, nor even annoyance. It was something that had obviously never happened. How *could* it? That's the point: it could never have happened. Not with Fenton Flaherty and

Hester Day. With his hands back on the wheel and his eyes narrowing down at the highway in front of us, with his blank features and his colorful and wooly Swiss Alps hat, he was none other than the white-trash poet. And always *had* been. Those hands grabbed hold of a girl the same way they'd flushed a toilet.

Maybe that's the only valid reason why we picked up the hitchhiker—to make sure that there was a diversion. I can't really think of why else Fenton would have pulled over next to him. It's not like we needed another extremely unrelated item for the contents of the camper.

"Make room, guys," Fenton said, "we're picking up this guy."

The stranger jumped a little at the sudden appearance of such an aggressively eager vehicle. The ski jacket that he held over his head slipped from his grip and he almost ended up stepping on it and slipping too, for that matter. It had been raining all morning and the ground was just aching for slapstick comedy. He caught his balance at the last moment and then looked over as we rolled to a stop. He was long and skinny with a tangled beard.

Fenton suddenly shifted back into gear. "Never mind. He seems to be some kind of Jesus freak."

My arm shot out and landed hard on Fenton's arm.

"Are you kidding? You can't drive off just because someone is a Jesus freak!"

Oddly enough, that was the first real thing I'd said to him since the "incident."

"I happen to have weird feelings about this guy," Fenton replied coolly, clawing my fingers off his arm.

"Weird feelings my ass."

We'd been rolling along the side of the road, but here, he came to another complete stop.

"I hate it when you say that," he said with one of those laborious sighs. "It's the most infantile way of counteracting an opponent's argument."

I had half a mind to crack open a smile. This was Philosophy Man, the way I'd known him before we were married—back at the library. Back when I'd watch him industrially work his way through the shelving systems. I never knew why he spent so many hours there, but I was impressed, I guess, by his completely senseless activities.

"Hester, are you listening?"

And this was him *now*.

"Look," I said, "you can't bring someone's hopes up like that and then just drop them."

"I *owe* this guy something? You want me to set up a trust fund for him while I'm at it?"

"Oh, shut up. How the hell do you know he's a Jesus freak anyway?"

"Are you kidding me?"

"He has a beard. Big deal."

"My dad is a Jesus freak. I know these guys. I can smell them across the fucking Atlantic Ocean."

"Yeah, I'm sure you specialize in that."

"You have a dad?" Jethro asked, looking up.

"Yes, I do. In case you didn't know, humans need to mate in order to produce children. It's highly unlikely that a female will produce a child asexually."

Jethro's eyes wandered. "Oh, like—"

"Yeah, let's not get into that right now," I said. "We have Jesus Freak here trotting up to the camper and we still haven't made a decision."

Fenton cast a glance at the figure with the ski jacket back over his head.

"What are you talking about? I already made a decision," he said. "I don't know what makes you think anything about it is going to change."

"Is this about your dad?" I asked. "You didn't get along with him or something and now you take it up with all Jesus freaks of the world?"

"I got along with my dad great. I just wouldn't pick him up if he were a hitchhiker." Fenton's eyes narrowed in on me. "What the hell's wrong with you anyway? Are you PMSing?"

"Oh please. What am I? A machine that can only have mood swings when its hormones are having a party?"

Somehow I couldn't keep my eyes on him.

"Okay, fine, we'll pick up the goddamn Jesus freak!" Fenton said. "Just don't blame *me* if he turns out to be a serial killer and we all end up in various little Ziploc bags in his fridge."

Jethro looked over. "How could somebody say something when they're cut into bits?"

"That's not the point," Fenton snapped.

"Yes it is."

"No, it's not. How would *you* know what my point is?"

"I'm just saying you can't talk if you're cut into pieces."

"Look, next time I want your forensic input, I'll pose the question to you directly."

We all stopped. There was Jesus Freak's face staring in at my window. His long hair was plastered against his forehead and ears, and his beard was loaded with rain. He was young enough not to be old, but I guess that all depends on how old you are. He looked to be about in his early thirties. You could tell by his face that he was probably a mountain climber. Maybe I'm just saying that because he looked healthy. He looked like he had more life in him than any of us in the camper. The kind of health that none of us could have had, the way we grew up. There was some kind of midsized-town filth clinging to us that had to be washed off in a baptism before we could ever glow like this hitchhiker.

I pulled down my window quickly. "You need a ride?"

"Holy shit, guys!" he said. His voice was mild and slow, and he overly enunciated everything, which made him sound pretty goddamn ridiculous. I nodded and he continued. He talked like an English teacher would talk to a beginner's class somewhere in Taiwan.

"Thanks! You have no idea how long I've been waiting here. People seem to be scared of beards or something."

"Yeah," I said, casting a dark glance at Fenton. "I know."

"So," I continued, "you want a ride?"

"I sure would appreciate it. Where are you going?"

I shrugged my shoulders. "Apparently Chicago."

"Right on. You guys have some space in the back there?"

"What for?" Fenton asked suspiciously.

"Just my luggage."

Fenton looked at me with irritation, and then as though it was too late anyway, he threw me the keys to the back. I got out into the rain just in time to witness the hitchhiker pull up something from the ground that appeared to be a cross big enough to nail a buffalo to. I didn't bother exchanging glances with Fenton. So he was right for *once* in his life. The hitchhiker was a Jesus freak. Big deal.

Unlocking the back of the camper for him, I couldn't resist asking innocently: "Are you a religious man?"

"I do what I can."

"Yeah, I can see that."

"People tend to think I'm a Jesus freak, you know. I think that's why people aren't picking me up."

"Mm-hmm. Well, you *are* carrying a cross around slightly larger than what most people would be willing to put up with."

"Maybe I am, but that's just one of my little quirks. Really I'm just a normal guy—law degree, parents still wanting to meet my wife, dreams about becoming a radio talk-show host. Blah, blah, blah."

"I guess that's pretty normal."

"Yeah."

"So the cross is just for fun?"

"I have people sign it. I live by the Bible—just like anybody else—just doing my bit. I'm probably no different from you or your friends up front."

The cross was now halfway in the camper. I climbed in and pulled from the other side, while Jesus Freak gave it a final push.

"Well, I can't argue with you about you doing your bit," I said, jumping back out, "but I'd be more careful about saying you're no different from us. We have quirks you don't even want to *know* about."

"Oh, I mean it. We're all human beings."

"You're a bold man saying that."

He began staring me down with intense interest. "You don't think we're all human beings?"

I rolled my eyes secretly. "Well, technically we are. Maybe that's the problem. The human race. Men, women . . . oh, fuck, I'm talking out of my ass."

It was embarrassing the way we were having deep conversations out in the back. This was seriously a terrible art film.

"Come on," I said, locking up, "people are only allowed to have these types of conversations with perfect strangers when they're shitfaced somewhere at five a.m. I think there's an actual law about that."

"You seem to be having a hard time with something," he said nonchalantly.

The rain fell around us and I stood frozen with the keys in my hand.

"What do you mean?" I asked, shocked.

"Well, something's wrong, no?"

The way he asked things was so endlessly blatant and innocent. It was playground curiosity. That was probably the only reason I wasn't offended; but, of course, I still made a pretense of being irritated.

"You sound like a shrink."

"Sorry," he said quickly. "I know I have no right to ask you something like that only three minutes after we've met."

I finished locking the door.

"On the contrary, you have the right to ask me any question starting right from the first second in which we met; but I don't have to answer any of them. Not even after we've known each other for ten billion years. That's the beauty of it all."

He nodded.

"Seriously, though, as far as I'm concerned I'm just a little spoiled brat. And if I say I have troubles I'm only flattering myself. Come on, let's get out of this rain."

I slammed the back door, and Jesus followed me up to the front.

QUESTION BEGS THE ANSWER

I DON'T KNOW how we thought picking up a hitchhiker would change anything—or divert our attention—because our attention remained plastered on everything we strove not to think about. Nothing changed in the department of graceless schoolyard feelings, except that now we had a total stranger sharing the place with us. And his cross.

"Duncan Clyde," said Jesus Freak, reaching out his hand to each of us.

"Hester," I said. "This is my cousin Jethro. And that's—my husband, Fenton."

He smiled. "Well, I'm glad to meet you all. I'm sure I couldn't have asked for finer company on this rainy day."

The radio began to play soft religious hymns, and we stopped talking. I'd lost track of where we were—although we had wasted so much time going nowhere in particular that I think we were still in Kentucky. We had drifted down quite a few strange winter landscapes. Little country roads that crawled through forests where obsolete graveyards grew between the trees. Lots of rain all day. Bleak gas stations, with terrible bathroom situations. Sometimes, we'd come across local gas stations—family-owned and -run—with neat little hot dogs turning slowly behind counters, and friendly ladies willing to give you advice on any subject under the sun, moon, and stars. Maybe I should have asked *them* about what to do. But who would understand? I didn't even really understand anything myself.

Evening. The headlights burrowed bright tunnels into the night. I'd woken up about an hour ago and decided to play dead. I just lay there and listened to how the radio cranked out lively tunes. Far too lively for the occasion. Jethro had fallen asleep and Duncan sat with calm eyes staring at the road.

"I wonder, Fenton," Duncan said all of a sudden, "could you pull over at the next gas station? I'd like to buy some peanuts— only if it's not a problem."

Fenton said "Sure," sounding like he meant to say something much less accommodating.

Soon we sat bathed in the bright lights of a Texaco station, watching Duncan scan the trail mix shelf in the store. He picked out each little package and turned it over, studying the ingredients with a meaningful stare, and then put it back. I realized this would take longer than anticipated. Fenton and I passed the time by staring out at people holding fuel pumps to their cars and yawning. Duncan called one of the cashiers over and they presently fell into a lively conversation about the trail mix stock. The silence in the camper became annoyingly ominous.

"Fenton," I began at long last.

"What?"

"I thought it was kind of an established fact that we didn't like each other. And that's not to say that we don't *appreciate* each other. Just that we don't like each other."

He looked over blankly. "Is that a question?"

"Who cares? I just want to know why we would make out like we did yesterday if that's the case."

"I dunno. Jethro was taking a piss. Seemed like the thing to do at the time."

That made me feel like scratching a long line across the hood of his car with those scissors we kept in the glove compartment for self-defense. But I guess I was too old for that. Or too sensible. Or too senseless. Something like that.

"Well," I said, reaching for the door, "I'm going to start smoking again."

I passed Duncan on the way to the store. He had two packs of trail mix in his hands and watched me closely as I walked by.

"What's wrong?" he asked.

"Nothing. I'm buying cigarettes."

"Sure?"

I stopped and frowned hard. "Sure I'm sure. I need nicotine in my body. Is that so weird?"

"No, it's not weird at all."

"Well, there you go."

"Sorry, I really didn't mean to make it sound like—"

"Oh, forget it," I interrupted him, waving my hand. "I'm just being obnoxious. Don't mind me."

It made me wonder when I got back in the car whether we all saw the first traces of disease and just did our best to pretend we were oblivious to it. Were things going terribly wrong? I looked over at Jethro's sleeping face. I've always loved the way you can stare at people when they're asleep. Watching their lips hang open in complete stupor while dreams and nightmares climb over their faces. Sleeping people seemed to be drowned in ignorance. It must be true what they say. Ignorance is bliss. As soon as you close your eyes, all relevant subject matter is cleaned off the slate, and you begin to run down corridors with green light filtering through from behind you. Evil takes on the form of witches and werewolves and dark translucent figures—and that's the way it ought to be, if you ask me. Who wants to deal with evil in the form of lawyers and politicians, love affairs and malignant tumors? In dreams everything is so much more worth your trouble. Trouble has style. In real life—well, *look* at it.

"I can take over the wheel if you guys want to get some sleep," Duncan offered.

"You got a license?" Fenton asked to my surprise.

"I do," Duncan said. "I mean, it's not *on* me or anything. But I did the test and all that, I'm just not good at keeping track of little plastic slabs."

Fenton turned the camper off to the side and pulled out the road atlas.

"You think you can handle this route?" he asked, pointing out the highways he had marked with a green highlighter.

Duncan squinted his eyes over the network of highways and, fondling his beard like a pirate, said, "Looks pretty straightforward."

For a moment Fenton hesitated. The keys dangled lifelessly in the ignition and it was doubtful whether he would clear the driver's seat or not. I imagined I could see a cold sweat over his forehead. I didn't think he'd go through with it. But he did.

He threw open the door and said, "Well, take good care of Arlene. I'll be in the back if you need me."

I admit I listened with an open jaw and not without thick blood trickling out of a wound somewhere. My husband had told me once that he'd rather "drive the camper off a cliff" than let me take over the driver's seat. So you'll have to understand that I was at a loss not only for words but also for thoughts when he handed over the keys to a random stranger without so much as flinching at the thought. Not just any random stranger—a guy that a few hours ago he was still reluctant to let into the car for fear of him being a serial killer. I couldn't believe it. He would risk Arlene— he would risk the whole worth of his life just to send me reeling. I shook my head. Well, maybe I didn't, but I should have, because I was at a funeral—our relationship (whatever it was) had died. Fenton and I were strangers and all the reasons why I imagined we got along seemed to have evaporated before my eyes.

We left Jethro sleeping in the front with Duncan and the road atlas. I didn't want to wake him up, and I knew if I brought him to the back he'd most likely wake up from the pan that I'd be slamming over Fenton's head.

"Don't tell me you're pissed off about Duncan driving," Fenton said when he had slammed the door shut behind us.

"Nothing is quite that simple," I said.

He rolled his eyes. "You *are* pissed off!"

"No," I said, walking past him and ripping the quilt off the bed. "I'm just bored to death with your ideals. I'm bored with your way of talking and your way of trying to prove whatever the fuck you're trying to prove to me. I'm bored of 'Transplant' and I'm bored of your asshole pretense."

"My asshole pretense?"

"Come on. You're not half the asshole you wish you were. You only keep it up for me. Today for lunch—you were as polite to that old waitress as a five-star-hotel doorman is to the millionaire ladies whose tips he depends on to feed his children."

"You think I'd create an alter ego for you alone?"

"Not just an alter ego—you've tailor-made an entire Mr. Hyde for me."

"You have a lot of nerve thinking that the whole world revolves around you."

"I was only talking about *you*—no mention of the whole world."

"Has anyone ever told you that you're a little brat, fresh out of kindergarten?"

"Plenty of people have. Has anyone ever told you that you're a sad cliché of a beatnik poet who's already being a cliché of some lame version of Lord Byron?"

Fenton didn't say anything, just watched me make a small bed for myself on the other side of the camper, where Jethro's sleeping bag was lying. He had his hands in his pockets and stared, lifeless and cold, just watching me like I was a science experiment clawing to the inside of my test tube.

"I'm getting a divorce from you," I said.

He could have been thinking a million different things, but I'll never know what any of them were. Nothing in his face had shifted. Not a muscle. Everything was cast in stone.

"On second thought," I continued, "why would I get a divorce? That would be a sad joke. All I need to do is walk away. This marriage started off fake; it can end just as fake."

After an uncommonly long silence he simply said: "Thought I'd never be able to breathe easy again."

I couldn't believe he could say something like that so effortlessly, with his hands in his pockets. His expression was so frank and eventless. How was I supposed to feel about that? I wanted to feel like ripping out his tonsils, but I couldn't. There was no derisiveness in what he said—not even any loathing.

"Well," I said, "you know there never was any point in worrying about that. You should have known that I would leave just as easily as I'd come—there never really was a question about that."

"How will you ever make it?" he said. "I'm afraid just to watch sometimes. I think every time you cross a road a truck is bound to mow you down."

That made me wonder whether he cared or whether he just didn't like the sight of roadkill. I decided not to ask and finished making my bed across the room on Jethro's sleeping bag. Yeah, I was divorcing my husband in true style.

I didn't know why I smiled. I sure didn't find anything about our conversation particularly amusing. It was maddening and sad, and then there was that part of me that still wanted to lodge the pan into Fenton's head. I didn't know anymore who was gaining and who was losing ground—or what exactly I was talking about for that matter. The outcome of the argument didn't seem to carry any interest to me. Not anymore. I wasn't after any kind of trophy, so I leaned over and turned out the lamp.

That Fenton and I were enemies never was much of a question, but I had suspected an ineffable loyalty nesting somewhere in a space between us that you couldn't point to. It had always felt strange to me to think that my enemy was one of the few people I could trust, but I liked the idea of this. I liked the idea of loyalty lying where it never was supposed to be in the first place.

Well, it wasn't fun to discover that I'd depended on figments of my own imagination for comfort. Especially not in a sleeping bag on the floor.

SOMEWHERE I'VE NEVER BEEN BEFORE

THAT NIGHT I froze my ass off and dreamt that I gave birth to a lizard. It was one of those endless nights when you are aware of every discomfort down to the ticking of another person's wristwatch, and all you can do about it is lie there like a corpse, too paralyzed to move a muscle or make an effort to cure the miserable setting of your bed. The morning plow. I began to consider my argument with Fenton from the night before, and the fact that today we'd go our separate ways lay across my mind like a struggling victim tied to a railroad track. Who knows—maybe we had no cause to even shake hands anymore. It was hard to tell the damage with just one glance at the lifeless battlefield in the morning light.

I got up and slid open the partition that separated the back of the camper from the front. Duncan and Jethro were in the process of laughing about something. They were listening to a live broadcast of a yodeling competition. The road in front of them was smothered in fog. Everything was so gray and peaceful, just like the morning of a divorce should be. The crackling of yodels from Japanese contestants blended seamlessly with the landscape. It gave the day a melancholic taste. And I think I might have been jealous to see people laughing helplessly over a yodeling competition, because *I* couldn't. I guess now I knew why so many people used to stare at me in dismay when I cracked up at something.

We pulled into a gas station at around eight thirty that morning to tackle the coffee machines. If you're on the road for this long you begin to realize that caffeine is the real reason your body works at all. Jethro took off running around the back of the building, just like kids are supposed to when you let 'em out of a car. Duncan took his cross out of the back to have a couple from Texas sign it. Fenton and I found ourselves standing in front of a coffee machine, waiting for our cups to fill. We tried to ignore each other, but that's always easier said than done. We didn't say anything—just stared at each other in suspicion.

We had that quality of never making sense to each other, and so we were always making up our own stories. We'd stare at each other and interpret expressions. We'd study each other's eyes and the way our lips were parted, the way we breathed and the way our eyebrows dipped over our eyes. We'd try and figure out by the coloring of our faces and the shadows under our eyes what we were trying to say. Sometimes we got a lot further that way than with talking. We resorted to techniques scientists use for studying new plant species. It was particularly bad that morning, of course, awkwardly dividing our stares between the streak of black chemical coffee filling paper cups and each other. Where are all the aliens when you need them? Why don't they ever attack innocent stores and fields and farmers when it would actually be of use?

Suddenly Fenton's wandering gaze froze on a shelf behind me.

"We're in Illinois, right?" he asked.

"Yeah," I said. "We should be, if Duncan drove most of the night."

Fenton left his coffee standing and brushed passed me to the shelf.

"They're selling shot glasses here that say Missouri on them."

He handed me the glass and we both studied it.

"Is that normal?" he asked.

I began to smile. "Not really all that normal."

It felt ecstatic, to realize you've been abducted by the Jesus freak that you picked up the night before. It felt glorifying—at least to *me* it did. It had that quality of making me feel freshly baptized. Cleaned, gutted, and bright to start all over again. These were the very fibers that life are made of! Although, I do believe Fenton's sentiments on the subject might have been slightly different.

"I'm going to kill that son of a bitch!"

"No," I said. "I'm sure he's got a perfectly sensible explanation."

Well, okay, "perfectly sensible" was maybe going too far. But he *did* have an explanation, and frankly, it was *better* than sensible:

"Well, when you guys were talking about going to Chicago, I started getting these bad vibes—and I mean they weren't just your average bad vibes, they were *real* bad. There just wasn't a way I could let you go on up there like you planned—not after you picked me up out of the rain and all. Now, I know I could have told you about all that back in Kentucky, but I had a feeling that if I told you right there, you might not have taken me very seriously. You might have considered me a nut or something— I'm not saying that's what you would have thought, but it *has* happened before."

"*What?*" Fenton cried. "What the hell are you talking about?"

I put my hand on his shoulder. "Calm down, he just got some bad vibes."

"Or you could call them 'energy flows' if you want to," Duncan said.

Fenton looked like he was being held up at gunpoint. "Excuse me, did a spaceship just land and drop me off here? What the hell is happening? *Vibes?*"

Duncan scratched his beard nervously. "I'm really sorry, guys, but this was the only way I could think of to stop you from going to Chicago."

"Tell me that you missed the exit or read a few wrong signs!" Fenton cried. "Tell me that you wanted to hijack the fucking camper for Christ's sake—just *don't* tell me that we're standing here right now because you picked up bad flows of energy!"

I took a step back so as not to flaunt my grin, which was shamefully out of place. I couldn't help it. Where do moments like this *come* from?

"Fenton, I—I wish I *could* tell you I was hijacking the camper, but why would I need a camper?" Duncan said quietly, and then his voice faded away.

The fog hung down so low that it touched the ground. The three of us stood a little removed from the pumps, smothered in the faint, icy drizzle. No one said a word for a few moments. There comes a point in absurdity where effort of any sort feels like a root canal, and you're better off just making friends with the occasion. This was one of those points. The pain drained from Fenton's face and left it blank. Even my grin melted into oblivion.

"You have every right to be riled up about this," Duncan said.

Fenton looked up. "I'm in Missouri because of your *vibes*. I think 'riled up' isn't quite the phrase I'd use."

"Well, feel free to use any word you want. I only wish you'd understand."

"Not likely," he said. "Just not likely."

We were up against a brick wall here. And it was getting cold.

"Fuck this. I'm going to get some coffee," Fenton said, apathetically turning back to the store.

"Wait!" I called. "You can't just leave! We don't even know where we're going from here!"

"I don't see why you guys bother asking *me* about it. My camper is obviously only a vessel to everyone else's private agendas."

"Really? So, I'll just work out the details with Duncan?" I asked hopefully.

"Fuck you."

He walked away.

"What's going on? You guys had another fight?" Jethro asked, coming up behind us.

"No. Well, maybe. I don't really know, it gets harder to tell every time," I said, "but you missed some interesting dialogue, that's for sure."

No decision was ever made in regards to a new itinerary, a new destination, or a new plan for the end of "Transplant." Fenton returned with his coffee, and we rounded up Jethro and got back on the road. Things were left hanging in the air, and I think we liked it that way. Duncan Clyde prevented Chicago from happening. He took away all reasons for anything. Now we were truly free. Absolutely no future in sight but the one that we created with each passing second of the wristwatch taped to the cabinet. We were in Kansas by noon, and not much later we were lost in an ocean of fields that looked orange in the light. The freeway had disappeared and we were on a slender dirt road. To our left and to our right the grass spread to bare horizons. Only a few skeletons of trees by the side of the road. At first there were lonely farmhouses that dotted the landscape, and barns with mailboxes, fences, and muddy courtyards; but these disappeared and left us stranded in the windswept plains of Kansas without even a cow for company.

None of us had talked for hours. The radio didn't pick up much more than static, and with Jethro napping, the silence was almost deafening.

Suddenly Fenton stepped on the brake and turned off the motor. We were cornered by nothingness. The road was so narrow at this point that if we'd encountered an oncoming car we would have been stuck.

"What's wrong?" I asked.

Fenton threw open the door and jumped out. "What's wrong? I don't know if you've noticed, but we're lost!"

I rolled my eyes to Duncan.

"I can't help but feel that this is all my fault," he said as we watched Fenton storm into the fields.

"Don't be silly," I said. "What's a writer going to do with a clean-cut life? He *needs* to storm off into the fields and look dramatic every now and then."

"Well, he looks awfully riled up."

"Big deal. I'd start worrying when he *doesn't* look awfully riled up."

I jumped out of the camper and crossed over into the field where Fenton stood, hands on his hips, staring intensely at the ground and taking deep breaths. I came up to him with a freshly lit cigarette.

"Fenton, I don't understand why you're a nonsmoker. With the amount of nervous breakdowns you have, it would do you a world of good to smoke."

He didn't move. And after a few moments he said, "You know we could mix sleeping powder in Duncan's drink at the next stop. He'll be out cold in no time, and we'll just leave him at the side of the road."

"Please don't tell me you carry sleeping powder," I said.

"In the glove compartment. Well, not *technically* sleeping powder, but these pills will knock an elephant out if you give him enough of them."

"Why do you have drugs like that in your glove compartment?"

"In case of a plane crash."

"In case a plane crashes *on* you, or in case you're *in* a plane that crashes?"

He stared at me like the last of his wits had just jumped the border.

"What the hell do you *think*? In case I'm *in* a plane that crashes, of course. How likely is it that a plane will crash exactly *on* me?"

"Fenton, we're in a camper in the Midwest—how likely is it that you'd be in a plane that's crashing while you're out here driving a motor vehicle?"

"What?"

We were obviously derailing here into the darker regions of Fenton's paranoia.

"Never mind," I said. "It doesn't matter. The point is we're not going to drug someone and then leave him in a ditch. Something about that smells illegal."

"Fuck illegal. He hijacked my camper."

"I thought we specifically established that he didn't hijack the camper. Didn't we have that whole conversation about vibes and all?"

"Who cares why we're here?" he said. "We're here—that's the point. And we seemed to have crossed over into another galaxy, because on this planet there aren't any freeways, there aren't any gas stations, no road signs—nothing."

"Are you freaking out because we're lost?"

He looked over at me. "You know, Hester, sometimes I feel I really want nothing as badly as to strangle you."

I patted him on the back. "I feel the same way about you sometimes."

We heard the door of the camper slam and soon afterward Duncan appeared by our side.

"Listen, guys, I know it seems like we're lost," he began hesitantly, "but as a matter of fact, we're not. There should be a farm coming up after that little hill over there. Shouldn't take us more than ten minutes to get there."

"You know this area?" I asked.

"Not particularly, no."

Fenton and I stared.

"So, how do you know there's a farm over that hill?"

He shifted his position nervously. "Well, fact is, I'm a little psychic. I didn't want to spring it on you guys earlier in case it made you feel even weirder."

"Yeah, it sure makes a difference when you pick out the right time," Fenton said.

Then he walked off, back to the camper, where Jethro was just in the process of sticking his head out the window.

"We need to find a bathroom somewhere really soon!" he called over.

ALL THEM PROPHETS ARE
DEAD AND GONE

PERHAPS EVEN weirder than having the hitchhiker tell us he's
psychic was the realization that he might be telling the truth. The
view from the top of the hill was much the same as it had been
from the other side. Kansas spilled all the way to the horizon; it
seemed to never end, even where the fields met the sky you were
certain things just continued right on completely unaltered. Only
the black branches of a single tree could be seen farther down
by the roadside. The sky was still gray and heavy, hanging over
fields that now looked more orange than ever. The wind hadn't
stopped blowing and pulled viciously at the grass. We sat and
squinted our eyes. This is where it would be decided whether the
Jesus freak was a lunatic or—worse than that—some kind of a
prophet. It made me think: what if all this time there really *was* a
God, and Jesus really did appear to people as a vision and point
at them with a ray of light and endow them with supernatural
powers? And all these people that we labeled "freaks" were really

the ones laughing at *us*? What if all my life I've lived on the wrong side of religion? There's a scary thought.

Jethro cut through my train of thoughts with a chainsaw.

"Duncan *is* psychic!" he yelled out, pointing into the distance. "Look!"

He was right. Outlined against the left-hand corner of the horizon was the dark shape of a barn.

"Oh please!" Fenton muttered. "Kansas is *littered* with barns. You can hardly move without brushing up against one."

"Yeah," I said, "except for the last two hours, huh?"

The farm grounds consisted of two barns and between them an old-fashioned house that had been whitewashed a long time ago. It looked like the wind had played with it and bent it out of shape a little. There were no neighboring signs of life. There was a little mailbox and a fence that neatly separated the farm property from the wasteland surrounding it, but that was it. It made you wonder whether the inhabitants ever realized that they were in the middle of nowhere. Probably not. Who knows? For them this might be a metropolis. A pair of plaster dogs sat on either side of the entrance to the yard, both of them staring to the right, which left my sense of symmetry horribly unsettled. There was also a whole army of miniature American flags—the ones on little plastic sticks that you push into the ground on the Fourth of July. Besides that and a garden dwarf lying with his face down in the ground, the yard was deserted and neglected. The porch was well swept and had one of those benches suspended from the ceiling by chains. In movies people are always drinking iced tea on those things.

"I think this is totally random and ridiculous by the way," Fenton muttered as we approached the front door.

"Jethro needs to pee."

"Well, Jethro can pee behind a bush. He's been doing it the whole trip. I don't see why he suddenly needs a toilet in an idyllic farmhouse."

Jethro screwed his face into obvious annoyance. "I'm not using any of those bushes. You can see through the branches."

"I don't see a line of people lining up to watch you pee."

"Well, why don't *you* pee behind the bushes if you think it's such a great idea?"

"Because I'm not the one with the bladder the size of an acorn."

"My bladder isn't the size of an acorn. Your *brain* is the size of an acorn!"

I rang the doorbell. Fenton and Jethro dropped the argument, and we all waited for the footsteps from inside to make their way to the door. Eventually the door swung open and we found ourselves facing a skinny, elderly man with black beads for eyes, overalls, a flannel shirt, and a baseball cap that said "Big A Auto Parts" on it.

"Who is it, Elvin?" a woman's voice echoed through the entire house.

Elvin turned and yelled back, "Well, I haven't had a chance to ask them yet, have I?"

Then he turned to us and cranked out a weird smile.

"Can I help you, folks?"

The way he smiled made him look like a Bible salesman with a hidden agenda. But once I explained that we were lost and Jethro needed to use the bathroom, he opened the door up wide.

"Oh, come on in. Come on in."

"Thanks."

Elvin's small, lean form dug through the dark hallway as he motioned for us to follow.

"When I was about nineteen, I lost my right leg in a fishing incident," he began out of the blue. "Now, my right leg might *look* real enough, but it's just about as fake as a leg can get."

We all searched for something to say, and one of us finally said, "Sorry to hear it, sir."

It was amazing how decent we all could act if we put our minds to it. One would almost believe we were civilized.

"Where are you folks from?" Elvin asked.

"Florida."

"No! You aren't friends of Jack, are you?"

"Doubt it," I said.

"Oh. Well, Jack arrived just yesterday from Florida—if that ain't a coincidence I don't know what is. Bathroom's right through there, son."

Jethro shuffled into the bathroom and the rest of us followed Elvin farther down the hallway into a large kitchen that overlooked the fields and an abandoned clothesline. There was an old lady standing by the counter chopping vegetables. She was probably in her early sixties, still kind of healthy-looking, but you could tell she probably had back problems or liver problems or whatever the hell it is the grandparents always tell you about when you have them on the phone.

"Lorna, these folks are from Florida," Elvin said, waving in our general direction.

Lorna smiled and scanned us over thoroughly. The way that lady looked you over, you knew she sucked every crime you ever committed right out of your pores, all the way back to the first cookie you ever stole out of a cookie jar. She never stopped smil-

ing, but her milky-blue senior citizen eyes made you feel like you
held a bloody ax in your hands the whole time.

"Oh, nice to meet you. You must be here for Jack. I think he
went out a short while ago," she said.

"No, they've never met Jack. They're just lost," Elvin answered
for us.

"Well, what a surprise. Before you know it, all of Florida will
be knocking at our door. Lord knows we can use the company.
Sit down, please."

We all sat down around the kitchen table like it was something
we had never done before. Elvin continued to stand there, kind of
clumsily, scratching his arm and watching us.

"Dear, what's the matter with your eye if you don't mind my
asking?" Lorna said, nodding over to me.

"Oh," I said, feeling the remnants of the bruise under my eye
with my hand. "I ran into a schizophrenic cashier over in Russel-
ville. He was normal up until it was my turn to pay for my milk.
When I got to him, he just jumped over the counter and tried to
strangle me. I was kinda lucky. I got away with a black eye."

The lie just pumped out of me. I was probably more surprised
than everyone else was about it. I know. Usually people lie to
downplay the outrageous nature of a truth; why I was doing the
exact opposite I couldn't tell you. I guess it was her questions.
They seemed loaded, and I didn't know how to dodge properly.
Hell, I didn't even know why I was dodging in the first place.

"Well, I suppose you really can't trust people anymore like you
used to," Lorna said. "I'll have to put something on it for you after
dinner."

"Thanks."

She didn't believe a word I'd said of course, but that was all right, because I wouldn't have believed a word of it either if I were her. Anything I could possibly have said would have sounded fishy anyway.

"Our dentist was arrested for making fake twenty-dollar bills last year," she went on. "Who'd have thought a dentist would make fake twenty-dollar bills?"

"Well, *I* wouldn't have thought of it," I answered.

"And me neither. And half the world wouldn't have," she said, pointing with her spoon at me. "That's exactly how it's done, you see. Everything is always done by those you'd least expect to have done it. If you keep that in mind, you'll be fine. You'll always be one step ahead of all the others."

I felt like I was cornered into an extremely bad script—you know, the kind where a group of rambunctious teenagers stumble into a farmhouse and end up being used as human sacrifices in the cellar by a slightly unorthodox Christian church congregation.

We didn't know what was going to happen to us; the farmhouse had swallowed us up, and our fate was nowhere within our reach. All we could do was sit there patiently, waiting to be digested, and eventually we'd probably be spat back on the road by these Lord-fearing, friendly, middle-of-nowhere people. As Lorna made us tea and told us some more about the dentist, I decided I better get the hell out of the kitchen before I fell on my knees and confessed to something I didn't do.

"I better go get some fresh air," I said, getting to my feet and feeling very awkward about it. "I have a lung condition and if I don't get regular amounts of fresh oxygen, I get asthma attacks."

"Dear me!"

"Yeah. I spent last Christmas in the hospital."

Apparently, I had lost the ability to say anything that contained truth in it.

Outside, the weather hadn't changed much. It was still winter. It was still cold. There was no Missouri fog anymore; the skies were clean but they hung low with the premonition of something gray. I wrapped my scarf carefully around my ears twice and stepped off the porch, feeling very helpless against the future. The light was becoming weaker and the wind was growing in strength. It was definitely the wrong time to open the little door in the white picket fence and take a walk into desolation. But of course, after having been fried by Lorna in the kitchen, I wanted to go as far down that little road as I could before either freezing to death or being abducted by rowdy hillbillies. I believe that officially this might be what the definition of "freedom" refers to—a desolate afternoon, with nobody on the road but you, and the grass dancing in the wind and your thoughts anchored somewhere where no one else's thoughts could ever be anchored. That's what it must say in the textbook.

Satisfaction was just in the process of sneaking up on me when I discovered a figure in the distance. It's a little disheartening to have to share all that land with another person just when you've decided that the whole of it belongs to you alone.

The closer he got, the more I was convinced I was going to pass him by like he was a ghost. He just didn't have any business being there. It was that simple.

Of course when we actually got close enough, I had to scratch that plan, because it just so happened that the stranger in front of me was the same one from the Kentucky gas station. We stopped and stared at each other as though there was a physical impossibility to this encounter. And there probably should have been

a physical impossibility. It didn't seem kosher that a chance encounter in middle-of-nowhere Kentucky should lead to an exact
duplicate encounter in middle-of-nowhere *Kansas*. Especially
since time appeared to have been cut out of existence. Had time
passed at all? We were facing each other with the same scarves
over our mouths, the same folds in our coats, the same cigarette
between my mittens, each strand of hair tugging in the same
piece of wind.

"How are you?" I began, sounding cautious.

"Fine. You?"

"Yeah, me too."

It was kind of hard to decide on what to say next.

"Well . . . this is weird," he said.

"Yeah, I'd have to agree with you on that."

Were we really going to get into conversations about where
we came from, where we were going, why we were here, where we
grew up, what school we went to? It seemed strange to be talking
about things that made sense when nothing else made sense.

"I'm sorry. Usually I'm good at making conversation," he
said.

"Me too."

Someone missed their cue here, and we shared a short silence
of nothing much to do with our hands or eyes, or anything else
for that matter.

I shrugged my shoulders. "We don't actually *have* to have a
conversation, you know. We could just walk on. It's not like we're
at a reunion or something."

"Well, yeah, but walking on might be harder to do than having
a decent conversation."

He was probably right.

"Besides, after meeting here like this, we might *have* to start arranging official reunions."

"All right, all right," I said, "we might as well introduce ourselves, then."

"I would have introduced myself last time actually, but I didn't think there was going to be a point to it."

"Now there's a point?"

"Well, it would give us something to say."

"I'm Hester."

He pulled his scarf down from his mouth and we shook hands.

"Glad to meet you. I'm Jack."

DIG A HOLE, DIG A HOLE IN THE MEADOW

J ACK AND I walked back to the farm together, feeling stunned. It was a little eerie trying to make sense of coincidence. How could it be that of all the people available we'd stumble right into his one-legged grandpa's farm? And as much as we would have liked to skip the whole ordeal of being astonished, you really couldn't help being impressed.

"Jack, do you believe that some deity upstairs is eating crackers and deciding what will happen next in our lives?"

He looked over with a subtle grin. "I don't know about the eating crackers part."

"But do you believe *anything* is going on up there?"

"I don't know. I hope so sometimes."

"Well, how do you explain things?" I asked.

"I don't always feel like I have to explain things."

"Yeah, but I'm talking about *weird* things. We picked up this hitchhiker the other day, and it turns out he's not only a Jesus freak, but he's also psychic on top of it. How do you explain that? Or how do you explain that we ran into each other twice within a week?"

"Fate?"

"I think there's too many weird aesthetics involved for all these things to be contributed to fate. You have to understand, my life's suddenly become a masterpiece. I feel like making popcorn, sitting back, and just watching the whole thing from a distance. Fate is too clumsy for that."

"You're right. It's probably luck."

I couldn't help smiling.

"Why are you looking so hard for someone to pin things on anyway?" he asked after a while.

"I don't know."

"If I were you, I wouldn't give the credit away to anyone else. I'd keep it. I'd say *I* was the culprit."

Now, there's a thought.

"I'm glad you'll be sitting with us through that dinner," I said. "Your grandma scares the shit out of me."

"Well, she has a knack for that."

To some extent I guess it was evident that Jack and I were in love. What fabric that love was made of was less evident. Maybe it was the love two Hungarians share when they meet accidentally in Hawaii. Two surgeons who have just successfully completed a heart transplant. Romeo and Juliet. Maybe it didn't even matter. Most definitely it didn't matter. It was nameless—probably even pointless. It was vague and none of us would ever open our mouths and mention it. I didn't think about it much, to be honest, but there was something about Jack that justified every minute of the day. You couldn't offer him up any complications.

He would abolish them. He'd point out the fool in you without ever once calling you a fool. Silences around him didn't beg for conversation; and conversations with him never left you thinking you shouldn't have said something.

Dinner was already served by the time Jack and I made it back. The kitchen was warm like an oven. The windows had steam on them and the air was thick with the smell of hot fruit trapped in pie crust. There was enough food spread out on the table for a whole football team, by the way, and I had a hell of a time trying to figure out how Lorna herself could have prepared it all. I'd read plenty of stories that revolved around healthy American farm life, but never once did I expect American farm life to be healthy in actuality. Actuality had never been anything but sickly in my eyes; it felt strange walking into three-dimensional proof of something so wholesome. Even the colors in the room were saturated like candy. I was certain all this would have died out back in the dust bowl. Complete strangers in overalls and aprons inviting us in to have dinner with them, offering us up their house for as long as we'd want to stay—it was all shamelessly idealistic. You couldn't help but feel ill at ease, because as far as I was concerned, perfection is always best friends with a whole congregation's worth of flaws.

"Well, I'm glad you ran into Jack out there," Lorna said, pulling out a chair for me. "I would have hated to think of you wandering around this area in the dark all by yourself."

"Oh, this area seems pretty safe," I said.

She looked at me kind of intensely. "But dear, it's never safe after dark *anywhere.* They proved it scientifically in one of those magazines, I forget which one."

"Oh."

Lorna smiled broadly. "It's just the way of the world. That's how the human race was made, and there isn't anything we can do about it."

"Can't you let the kids eat without talking about the end of the world?" Elvin said, shaking his head.

"I'm not talking about the end of the world, Elvin. I'm talking about common sense. No one uses common sense anymore these days—especially when it comes to safety."

"Duncan is psychic, though," Jethro chimed in. "He could see everything bad that's going to happen way before it happens. Right, Hester?"

"Oh, definitely. Duncan's a true psychic."

Duncan blushed. "Well, I'm just a little more sensitive to the environment than most people."

"Oh," Lorna said. "Isn't that fascinating?"

I shifted my attention back to the plate in front of me and began to eat, wishing someone would crank up a new conversation about something I couldn't partake in. Something like hunting licenses or fly-fishing or tractor engines. Anything that would leave me to the potatoes on my plate. We hadn't eaten a good meal since the beginning of time—at least that's what it felt like. To have something so colorful and perfect steaming into my face melted all concerns about love, hate, and the end of the world. The table fell silent and for a moment there was peace on earth. All that could be heard was the silverware against the porcelain and the music from the television that was set up in the corner, playing vibrant commercials of SUVs speeding down desert highways.

"Lorna, this food is mind-blowing!" Duncan announced with a groan that didn't quite belong at a dinner table.

"Isn't that sweet of you," she said.

"I *mean* it—I don't think any words ever uttered by a human being could do justice to the glaze on this potato. And I'll swear by it."

"You sure know how to make a girl feel special. You must have them lining up at your doorstep!"

"Well, I don't *have* a doorstep actually."

"You don't have a doorstep?"

"I'm on a special mission, you might say. I'm getting to know my country."

I glanced up from my plate and caught Fenton rolling his eyes. I winked at him, and then noticed Jack looking over. My face erupted in a blush, and suddenly I no longer knew how to scoop up food or take a sip of water, how to swallow or how to chew. I could feel my cheeks just about burn off my face, and there was nothing I could do but sit there, well aware of the blatancy with which I had to swallow my fluster. It took a lot of willpower on my part to look up from that plate again, and the strange thing was, when I finally did, I was confronted with my senior yearbook picture. Right there on the television screen. That was the picture that my mom had made such a fuss about because my hair wasn't plastered to my head with cement.

The picture on the television screen abruptly cut to a news lady looking solemn as she stared us down. She said something about Hester Day being missing from her home since 4:00 p.m. last Friday, and that her ten-year-old cousin Jethro had disappeared with her. They showed a picture of him too. It was black-and-white and he was midblink, with his hair parted the way it was when I first saw him. Even in strange black-and-white snapshots, it was clear that he represented a dying species of childhood.

All dinner sounds had given way to absolute sterility. All faces had grown into still lifes. My fork dropped from my hand and hit the plate, sending a slab of carrot across the table. It landed on Elvin's glasses, slid off, and then fell into his lap.

Next, there was my mother standing outside our house with Margaret and Uncle Norman beside her. A little behind her stood my dad and Hannah. They all stared as though they were watching a casket being lowered into the ground. Made you want to wipe your eyes with a lace-trimmed handkerchief.

"This has come as such a shock to us," my mother was saying. "I don't know what we did wrong."

Her eyes were blurred with tears and her hair sat in perfect helmet-mode; her clothes were pressed and dry-cleaned and she wore her pearls and her American flag pin. My mother idolized television. She was probably shitting in her pants from ecstasy right then. I couldn't help but feel a shudder about the fact that someone could be so desperate for something so exceptionally pathetic. Can anything get lonelier and more depressing than the ideal of national television?

"Well, we always knew there was something wrong with her," my mother continued, leaning into the microphone. "Hester didn't develop properly. She's always had trouble adapting. She has strong tendencies to irrationality and violence, but we just didn't conceive that she would be taking drugs behind our back. Like any parents, we didn't want to confront the possibility of our own daughter doing what we'd only seen people do in movies. With the state of her condition it was of course inevitable that something like this would happen, but I think we didn't want to believe it for a long time. We could not have known that—that it would come to this."

My mom started to cry again and the camera swung over to Margaret, who was wearing her shorts and a sturdy olive-green, outdoors-type of hunting or fishing jacket—the kind that people wear on the Discovery Channel when they're standing somewhere in Alaska pointing out otters and albino rabbits and whatnot.

"Mrs. Montgomery, how do you feel about your son being kidnapped by a close relative?"

Margaret looked blank. "It's certainly better than him being kidnapped by a stranger. And you know, I wouldn't want to jump to conclusions here. I mean, we can't really know *what* happened. All we know is that they disappeared."

"Are you optimistic about his recovery?"

"Oh, I think I am. I've never given God a reason to have a quarrel with me. And I can tell that just as you are standing in front of me right now, Jesus is standing beside Jethro."

I don't think any of us could help looking out of the corners of our eyes over at Duncan sitting next to Jethro.

The screen cut back to the news lady in her pink blazer, who asked the viewers to please dial the 800 number on the screen if they should have any information on either of the missing persons. It's strange the way television works. One minute you're watching news reporters tell you all about kidnappings, murders, forest fires, bombings, and floods, and the next minute you're watching some clean-cut lady with a ponytail and a jogging suit fawn over a new brand of deodorant. It cuts you out of time and space, making you the citizen of a strange land; and the place we all found ourselves in just then was probably the strangest yet.

I didn't know exactly what the right thing to do was after having been freshly baptized a kidnapper—on national television. I returned the stares with little hope of setting things straight.

I knew well enough how people worship anything a television set will say. I knew that the gospel truth didn't come from any Bible—it came from news networks. Any way you looked at it I was just about fucked.

"Well," Lorna said with a slow frown, and then stopped. She looked vacantly at the food sprawled across her dinner table.

Apparently nobody felt they could improve on that statement. It was bad enough being labeled a criminal, but without a reaction, how do you defend yourself? I felt a deep lethargy setting in. My paranoia of the old lady had peaked, and all I could think to do was shrug my shoulders. I wanted to argue, but I didn't know where to begin.

"Well," I said, standing up like I was about to propose a toast. "I'm sorry to have sponsored such a uniquely awkward moment. It really doesn't belong in this kitchen. I'm sorry."

Still nothing from anybody. So I decided to add an afterthought.

"And for what it's worth I didn't kidnap anyone. Maybe it's true that I have trouble 'adapting.' I don't know. I don't know what that means, to be honest. I guess I've had trouble adapting to assholes, but then I always thought that was a good thing."

Lorna made some sudden noise by piling empty dishes onto one another and stretched a smile across her face that looked a little painful.

"Well, who wants dessert?"

"Oh, no, I think we'd better get on the road," I said.

"I'm not sending anyone back on the road before breakfast, I don't care *who* you kidnapped," she announced sternly.

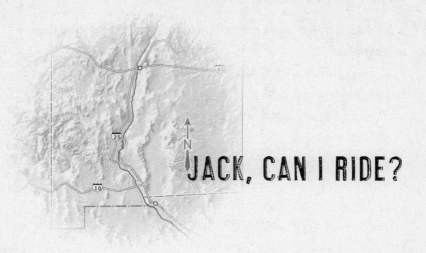

JACK, CAN I RIDE?

LORNA'S HOSPITALITY felt a little like a freight train. There was no way of avoiding it—it came out of nowhere and flattened you into resignation. I didn't want to stay, and I was pretty sure the others didn't want to stay either. And yet, after a hearty Monopoly game we found ourselves deposited in a guest room with a very blue theme. Blue enough to make the hair on your neck stand on end. I'm pretty sure Lorna and Elvin would have sooner sawed off their arms before letting us get back on the road in the storm that, according to the weatherman, was going to tear through Kansas that night. It was a sweet gesture, I guess, but it somehow didn't feel like it.

The good news was probably that nobody had commented on the kidnapping any further. Or maybe it wasn't such great news. In a way I wished somebody would have thrown a fit—something that I could have grabbed on to—but with nothing at all, I slipped right off and hit the ground. I wish I could explain how strange it felt to be sitting in a room decorated with porcelain geese, remembering every three minutes that apparently you are a drug addict who broke the law by dragging a kid into the back of a camper.

"These ruffles are making me nauseous," I said, sitting up in bed while Fenton played dead beside me.

"You gonna say something?" I asked after a while of silence.

"About the ruffles?"

"About anything. Seems to me we haven't argued in an awfully long time."

"Hmm."

"Maybe you'd like to comment on a certain national news report."

He shrugged his shoulders. "I don't really know where to begin."

"I wouldn't mind you not beginning at all, to be honest. I just think it might be bad for your system if you don't say anything. You might get constipated."

"What do you want me to say?"

"Whatever you want."

He sighed, just like he used to back in the days of the library when I came over to his table and seated myself without invitation.

"Hester, I could explain to you all about how stupid you are— packing a kid into the back of my camper without telling anyone. In fact, I was going to take you aside downstairs, but I decided not to. I figured the most irrational thing to do was to keep on playing Monopoly—get as many hotels as I could on Park Avenue—but that's exactly what I felt like doing."

"Why?"

"Because you exhaust me, Hester. Every day you drop something new in my lap—a little fat kid, some Jesus freak, a felony. I just wanted a holiday. I wanted to play some goddamn Monopoly and beat Elvin's ass. Is that too much to ask?"

I thought a while. "Hell, if I'd known how Monopoly unwinds your nerves I'd have bought you a game a long time ago."

"I'm not kidding."

"Yeah, I know. The funny thing is, I'm not kidding either. I'm scared of all those people across the country, ready to call that number."

He groaned. "Our first night in a real bed for about two weeks and you wanna talk?"

"I have insomnia. Excuse me if I'm a little anxious after being televised across the country as a child abductor."

"Come on, we all know you couldn't even abduct a *newt*, let alone a kid."

"I could abduct a kid *any* day, and I'd even go so far as to say I could abduct a newt."

"Well, I guess our opinions differ in that respect."

I shook my head. "It's not like you to take this lying down— you know that, right? How can you be so anal about things like how we fucking sit on your seats in the camper, and when *this* happens you just wanna sleep? Aren't you supposed to be strangling me right now or something?"

"I'll do it tomorrow."

I rolled my eyes. "Yeah, if you could, please, that would be grand."

"I can't believe you just said 'grand,'" he said.

"Well, I'm sure you'll get over it."

There wasn't any point in carrying on the conversation. Fenton was obviously more dead than alive. Maybe I really *had* exhausted him with the way I bent his existence around. I, in any case, found

it excessively hard to try and be unconscious under the circumstances. So I searched for my pack of cigarettes and left Fenton and
Jethro sleeping. The house was enormous in its own way, and as
a stranger in the dark it was next to impossible to remember how
to get to the front door. I slowly made my way down the hallway,
along the banister, remembering a Bob Dylan song:

*"And I wish I were on some Australian mountain range. / Oh, I
wish I were on some Australian mountain range, / I got no reason to
be there, but I imagine it would be some kind of change."*

I'd have given my right hand to be on some Australian mountain range.

"Where are you going?"

I turned and found Jack standing in a doorway, fully dressed,
with his eyes squinted out into the blackness.

"I'm trying to find the front door," I whispered back, holding
up my cigarette.

He closed the door behind him and motioned me to follow.
And that's how we ended up sitting on the front porch in the
dead of night and winter. If you sit on a porch with anyone at
night, you can't help but feel like you'd better say corny things,
but since there was no sunset or lemonade at hand I thought it
was okay to ignore this rule.

"I've never even taken drugs," I said.

"Me neither," he said, shrugging.

"Not for any other reason than the thought of it boring me.
Really. I don't even have anything noble to show for my abstinence
from drugs except disinterest. The thought of vegetating along in
Florida, and everything revolving around smoking weed or taking
whatever pills, powders, or liquids are cute or fashionable at the
time just seemed about as miserable as it gets. I mean, all these kids

are always wanting to rebel, which is okay, I guess, but how is taking drugs a rebellion anyway? Something that everyone and their
mother is doing? Might as well smother myself with true white
picket glory right from the beginning. Seriously—how can you
technically rebel by doing something that is the norm? And then
there are the parents, always wanting their kids to be lawyers and
doctors and marry rich people. I don't really see how any one of
these apparent extremes is worse than the other."

I took a short break to take another drag of my cigarette, while
nervously bouncing my leg up and down.

"Anyway," I continued, "I didn't want any part of any of it. The
only kind of high I ever wanted was to embed myself into situations that are surreal. That's all. I grew up being bored. I wanted
the opposite. But the *true* opposite, not the fake bullshit that millions of teenagers migrate through every year."

I looked over at Jack. "I'm sorry. I'm rambling like I've just
downed my fourth shot of vodka."

"I don't mind. You have a good vocabulary."

"I'm just so sore on this subject. You have no idea how often
my mom has paraded my filthy habits around town. It sucks after
a while, especially when my habits aren't even that filthy. But I
need to stop talking."

"I said it's okay."

"No, it's not," I said, annoyed at myself. "We agreed before that
we weren't going to go into all the obnoxious details of our lives."

"Well, I never really expected your obnoxious details to be so
engrossing."

"Thanks," I said, smiling a little.

"I'm not trying to flatter you, Hester, but your views seem all
right from over here."

"Really?"

"Yep."

After a short silence I said, "Am I really fucked now, do you think?"

"Well, not literally, but maybe metaphorically a little bit."

I smiled again.

"Can I ask you one more thing?" I said.

"Okay, one more thing."

"Can my mom really annihilate everything I managed to create just by crying on TV?"

"Probably," he said. "But then again, I'm sure you can keep her from annihilating it somehow."

"I'm glad you're sure about that. I'm not sure about anything anymore."

I could see he didn't feel like answering me. Jack wouldn't spare you any sympathy—he'd laugh at you before he'd feel sorry for anything you could possibly say, and that made conversation with him well worth it, because incidentally, I've always preferred being the perpetrator rather than the victim. We smoked together silently for a while, and all around us the storm swept across the farm grounds.

"Don't give me that look," he said out of the blue.

"What look?"

"You've got one hell of a conscience tattooed over your face."

"Don't you think I've got good reasons for a conscience?"

"Yeah, but *everyone* has good reasons for having a conscience."

"Maybe they do."

"Even if you *killed* somebody, that look wouldn't get you anywhere. Anyway, you didn't kill anybody. You just kidnapped a little kid."

In case you're wondering, one didn't need to *kiss* Jack to feel incestuous. Having a perfectly decent conversation about nothing that even borders on the land of lust would do the trick, and leave me feeling a little guilty. Needless to say, talking to him was the good kind of incest. We must have been sitting out there for close to an hour, talking about things that really didn't matter much any way you looked at them. We had a whole love affair made out of nothing within that hour. We married, had kids, and grew old together just sitting on those steps. When we finally put our fingers into an empty cigarette box, there was officially no reason left to be sitting in the cold. So slowly and reluctantly we got up, ready to return to lives that had time and reality in them.

"You better wake up your friends and get going tonight," Jack said just before we entered the house again.

I looked at him a little surprised. "Why?"

"Because Lorna's probably going to call the police first thing in the morning. That's just the kind of person she is—sweet but paranoid. She'll make you food one night and then call the police the next morning just to make sure she's in good standing with Jesus."

"Are you kidding?"

"No. I wouldn't get up in the middle of the night just to kid you about something like that."

"Why didn't you tell me until *now*?"

He smiled. "Because if I'd told you right away, we wouldn't have had that whole conversation."

I closed my eyes for a second, but when I reopened them, Jack still stood there, waiting patiently for me to stop trusting my fate to black magic.

"Well, shit," I said.

"Don't worry. Nothing's wrong yet. Years from now you wouldn't trade all this for anything. Trust me."

Fenton wasn't very thrilled about having to leave the bed in the middle of the night, but he cooperated. I expected worse. I realize that I always expect worse from Fenton. Did that make him more harmless, or did it simply mean that my imagination was easily agitated?

As for Jethro, he was a little groggy at first, but when I explained to him all about Lorna and Elvin being aliens disguised as humans and that they had notified their home planet for a spaceship to pick us up for medical experiments in the morning, he brightened up.

"Really?" he asked eagerly.

"Yeah. We have to leave now. Fenton's already starting up the camper."

"What about Duncan?" he asked as we made for the door.

"Duncan will be all right. Lorna likes him—they're not going to run any experiments on him."

"How do you know?"

"Well, he's psychic, remember? He'd know about everything way before it would ever come close to happening."

You have to be quick with kids. Mostly they're about ten steps ahead of you, like in chess. And even when you think you've taken the king, they still squint at you.

"Come on, honey," I said.

When we got to the porch there was that odd feeling of not knowing how to end an acquaintance.

"Jethro, why don't you run ahead and get in the camper," I said. "I'll be there in a second."

I loved the way Jethro took things literally. He jumped off the porch and sprinted into the darkness, leaving me and Jack behind with a few sensitive seconds to lay it all out on the table.

"Well, what can I say? I'm sorry I had to bring all this shit to your farm," I said.

"'Bring shit to the farm.' That sounds like an idiom."

"Yeah, it does," I said, breaking into a smile.

"I'm sorry," he said, "I want to say something more meaningful, but I don't know what."

"I'd rather we skipped all that too."

"Well, then let's skip it."

"Okay."

Having taken the need for significance away, it felt almost unbearable *not* to expound on feelings and regrets.

"I just feel like I dragged a dead rat into your home or something," I continued.

"Don't worry about the dead rat."

"And I really want you to know that I'm not usually this annoying. I've never PMSed in my life, and now it seems I'm making up for all those months of peaceful bleeding."

I looked up at him and realized I was being unnecessarily explicit. Although, it seemed to me that this moment had no rules. We could let it go by like the last pages of any cheap romance story written by some pink-haired lady, or we could give it class. We could let it go any old way we wanted to.

"Well, just promise me if you ever see my mom on television again that you'll watch it like a Monty Python episode?"

"Okay."

"And you'll always take my side and remember that she's a lunatic?"

"You have an adorable way of being paranoid, Hester."

"Thanks."

There's something thrilling about being complimented on new grounds.

"You better get going. Lorna gets up at around five thirty in the morning," he said.

I held out my hand and he shook it.

"Do you think we'll ever meet again?"

"Probably."

"Okay. Well, bye."

"Bye."

That was all there was to the ceremony. It was an understatement, obviously. We should have said something to shatter time and space, but there is something comfortable about simplicity. Emotions and eloquence can be a pain in the ass sometimes and only end up getting in the way of how simple things really are. I shook his hand and then made my way down the porch steps. I did wipe my eyes quickly as I walked through the dark to reach the camper. No more Jack, no more Jesus Freak, no Lornas or Elvins—life was stripped down to the bare minimum. Everything was about to continue just as it had started. Fenton, Jethro, and Hester.

We drove off that night with another Christian radio program blurting out advice and hymns. I talked a little with Jethro about the aliens, until his head got heavy and landed unconsciously on my shoulder. Fenton refused to take part in the conversation. When he was annoyed, he liked to make sure that the air around him smelled of irritation. I, of course, didn't give a shit. I had bigger fish to fry.

But I never stopped wishing I could have had Jack around for eternity to remind me of just how easy things really are. How we insist on crafting complications to our personalized standards.

SUN WENT DOWN

WAKING UP the next morning felt like waking up after a night of bad and loud karaoke. And as the day winds on, the little crumbs of memory keep trickling in, reminding you of all the different ways in which you were an ass.

All of us were lying on the front seat like exhausted fish waiting to be bought at a market—and that's probably how we felt too. Fenton's face was lying hard against his windowpane. His eyes were pressed shut as though with effort; he had that quality of always looking like he had just died a violent death when he slept. Jethro's feet were in my lap and the rest of him was outstretched on the seat. I was slumped against the other window with my head on my chest and my hair streaming down over my stomach.

I pulled myself up slowly, conscious of every bone in my body. My mouth tasted dry and the bruise around my eye was pulsing. I stared out the window and wondered if it was still morning—it could have been past noon, but it was hard to tell. The sun was weak and hidden behind layers of clouds. We were parked between two barren trees, a few yards off a country road. There weren't any houses in sight.

I reached across the seat and pulled at Fenton's coat sleeve. His eyes opened so immediately that it made me flinch.

"Please tell me that yesterday was a bad dream," he said.

"Sure. If you tell me the same thing."

That right there meant that it had most likely not been a dream. We said nothing more and turned back to our respective lives. Seemed like we intermingled less than ever. Fenton fumbled with the key until the camper coughed itself back to life, and we got on the road again. I wanted to look over at him and just stare, but I kept my eyes on the road before us. It had been one of my favorite pastimes to watch Fenton when he was focused on something. Just watching his eyes move and the thoughts crawling over his features; but now for some reason it seemed like that would be illegal. I had dragged him into my own personal wonderland, and what he had dragged me through was far more vague than any wonderland could be. I had been convinced I hated him, I had been convinced I loved him, I had even been convinced it would be impossible to feel anything but indifference for him.

"Where the heck are we going anyway?" Jethro finally demanded after about two hours of silence.

"I don't know where we're going, Jethro."

He looked a little annoyed. "Aren't we going to make a plan?"

"I think we should," I said. "Where are we going, Fenton? What's our plan?"

"*I* should know?" he said.

"You're driving."

"I'm going down the only road in *sight*. That doesn't mean shit."

"Well, it's your camper," I said sullenly. "Whenever I open my mouth in regards to itinerary I feel like you're going to toss a hand grenade over here. I wasn't going to offer this time."

"You're not making it all that easy for me to get from point A to point B, you know," he said. "I *had* a plan to begin with. I can't make up plans as fast as you derail them."

"Well, I'm sorry for being the sole reason your life is fucked up beyond apparent repair. But I think we should have some kind of a plan, regardless."

"My plan right now is going down the only road that we have at our disposal. If you want me to cut through the fields or something, let me know."

I gave him a dark look. "Well, if you're gonna follow that road till the end of eternity, you'll have to set me down somewhere along the way."

"Just tell me where."

We were obviously up a stump and we both fell silent. Jethro crossed his arms and put his feet up on the dashboard forcefully.

"Can we stop for some coffee soon?" he asked.

And then an oversized bird came out of nowhere. I imagine the bird was on some routine flight, thoughts far off, tangled up in nonsense, when a strong current of air sucked it from its course and splattered it with all its force at an unsuspecting camper. Either that, or the bird felt particularly suicidal that day. In any case, it was suddenly all over our windshield. I can't remember there being any noise; in fact, as far as I'm concerned, all noise evaporated entirely from the face of the earth for a matter of a few long seconds. Fenton's hands slipped off the wheel, the camper took an unintentional left, and we sped into oncoming traffic—except, of course, that there was no oncoming traffic. The road lay desolate between the dull Kansas fields.

Fenton pushed the brakes hard just as we were driving into a ditch. We landed on the dashboard and the bird slipped down from the windshield and somewhere to the left.

"The bird!" Jethro called. "Check if it's still alive!"

Jethro was the only one who always wore his seat belt. Consequently he was the first one on his feet.

"Jethro," I said, "I think it's dead."

He climbed over my lap and threw open the door. "How do you know?"

Before I could answer he had disappeared from sight.

The camper was all right. The bird was dead. Fenton had a small cut on his forehead that dyed a few strands of his hair red. I had a bruised arm. And Jethro was shattered about the animal death.

"Jethro, the bird probably led a real shitty life. I'm sure wherever the hell he is now, he's having a ball."

"You can't say that for sure, though," he answered.

We both stared at the battered bird as it was lying wide-eyed on the side of the road.

"Well, that's true. But looking at him I'd say he led a pretty moral life, which means he's probably going *up* and not down."

Jethro wiped away a tear and shrugged his shoulders. "Who even knows if all that crap exists?"

"Personally, I think he's going to be reincarnated."

"What do you mean? Into a new bird?"

"Yeah, or even into a bobcat or something."

He looked up, surprised. "A bobcat?"

"I guess it could be reincarnated into *any* medium-sized animal."

"What if he wants to be an *elephant* in his next lifetime?"

Trying to cheer up a kid about a small animal's death was a lot harder than I anticipated.

"I'm not really too familiar with the laws of reincarnation, to be totally honest."

It was freezing and my fingers were turning white in the wind. Our breath was dancing before our eyes, and I was trying with all my might not to remember that millions of people all across the country knew my name, my face, my hometown, my family, even my drug history, about which not even *I* knew anything. But then there was Jethro, wearing one of those corny Christmas sweaters that we'd picked up at the thrift store in Clarksdale. His black hair dancing in the wind and his large eyes staring in devastation at a little lump of feathers at our feet. There must have been something about this bird if it had the power of getting a kid like this to mourn its death.

"You know," I said, "I'm pretty sure if his willpower is strong enough he can be reincarnated into whatever he wants, including an elephant."

Jethro didn't answer, but I could tell it gave him some peace of mind to know that the bird's reincarnation wasn't restricted to medium-sized animals.

"Are we done staring at the dead bird?" Fenton said as he came up behind us.

"We can't just leave him here," Jethro said.

"There's no way in hell you're taking that thing into the camper."

"Why would I want to take a dead bird along with us?" Jethro asked.

"Because that's what kids *do.* They take weird shit into cars."

Jethro rolled his eyes. "We need to *bury* him. Right over here where he hit the ground, and we're going to have to put a cross there too."

"We're not burying any goddamn bird," Fenton said, turning back to the camper.

"Yes, we are," I snapped. "We're going to bury every single goddamn bird we hit!"

"No, we're not."

"Yes, we are."

"No, we're not."

"Yes, we are!"

Suddenly we found ourselves at the culmination of our entire relationship. High noon had come out of nowhere, and I could feel the hot dust crawling over the saloon porch, despite the fact that we were in a Kansas winter. I could feel the twisted curiosity of onlookers behind doors and windows, even though we were the only human beings this side of the horizon. Somewhere at the very back of my mind I found it kind of a pity that this moment had been sponsored by a bird flying into our windshield.

"Can I have a word with you behind the camper, please?" I said to Fenton.

"Sure."

Behind the camper, I turned to face Fenton and opened my mouth. Everything just came out faster than I could think it up.

"We're burying the bird," I said, hands turning into fists. "And your sorry ass is not going to stand between me and that burial. I'm sick and tired of asking you for permission every time I need to take a breath, every time I want to open my mouth, every time I need you to pull over so that I can use the lavatory. I can't even look at you anymore without feeling completely paranoid. What contract did I sign when I fucking married you, Fenton?"

"That's kind of what I'd like to know too," he said dryly.

This time neither of us would back down until one of us snapped like a twig.

"Oh, Fenton, we already know that I'm chronically getting us waist-high into shit. So I'm bad luck. What else is new? Don't you remember, when we set out on this trip, we *knew* we were getting ourselves into some kind of full-blown disaster. We were obviously craving it, or else we never would have so happily taken off that night. That next morning would never have been as perfect as it was. We didn't just crave it; we needed it."

"Who cares about all that subconscious 'wanting' and 'craving' and 'needing' shit? The fact is that you hid your cousin in the back and now we're running from farmhouses at three in the morning."

"So what? You think *anyone's* future is all neatly written up for them in some filing cabinet? You think I had any idea you were randomly going to make out with me on the car seat just like that?"

I must have thrown him off. The rage bleached out of his expression and for a few seconds he was deflated. Of course the fact that I had thrown him off threw me off in return, and neither of us could hit on anything more to say. We stood very still with our tongues suddenly lying paralyzed and heavy in our mouths.

"The point is," he began freshly, "I'm getting into that camper and I'm driving off. You can either get in it too, or you can bury the bird. It's up to you."

"I'm burying the bird."

In case you haven't noticed, the bird was more than just a bird at this point. It was a monster of significance.

Walking away, he said, "Well, don't tell me I didn't give you a choice."

"I hope I'll never have a chance to," I called after him.

Before he drove off he threw my coat and scarf out the window, just as we had agreed he must do if he ever dropped me off again. I watched them land on the ground and realized I could never hate Fenton. He had a network of indiscernible morals. It was hard to come in contact with them, but they were there.

As the camper pulled off, it revealed Jethro, still standing by the roadside with the bird at his feet. He watched the camper disappear over a mound and then turned toward me for an answer. Sense always flooded my conscience about two and a half seconds too late.

"Come on, let's bury the bird," I said.

"Where'd Fenton go?"

"Don't worry about him. He'll be back."

"Where'd he go?"

"I don't know. There must be a land where all the drama queens and psychotic writers storm off to whenever they need to create a scene."

He looked at me, puzzled. "You guys are really weird, you know?"

"Yeah," I said, putting my hand on his shoulder. "I know."

We decided on a good spot for a burial and got to work. The ground was hard, and digging a hole for a bird corpse was more work than I had initially imagined, especially since we were using sharp pieces of rocks for a shovel.

"I'm never going to marry," Jethro said out of the blue. "But if I do, I'm only going to fight with my wife about things like food or what TV channel we're going to watch."

"Those are probably the best things to fight about anyway."

Just then we heard the motor of a car humming in the distance. It didn't come from the direction Fenton had taken off into. It came from the other side. I turned and waited for it to come into view. My heart began to beat faster for some reason. Maybe I thought it would be Lorna catching up with us. I'd never been so paranoid about an old lady before. The car finally appeared, and when it came close enough for me to distinguish the shape and color, I thought I'd pass out cold. Unfortunately, I didn't. Life always seems to go on without anesthetic when you least want it to.

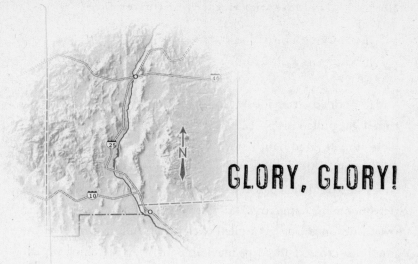

GLORY, GLORY!

OF COURSE it was a cop car. Anything other than a cop car would have been downright bizarre. It began to slow down because two kids kneeling by the side of the road with nothing around them is as good a reason as any for a cop to pull over. Jethro and I watched the car roll to a stop in front of us with dead expressions. My heart came up my throat and lay in my mouth, pulsing heavily.

"Hey there!"

He waved to us from his car. He was kind of tall, not overweight, just a little pregnant-looking around the guts—enough to make his clothes struggle. It took him a while to get out of his car. He was one of those officers who approaches leisurely and is clearly thinking of witty things he can say—even in the middle of nowhere.

"Hey," I said.

He came over and watched us for a while.

"What are you kids doing out here?"

He waited so long I thought he'd never ask.

"Just burying a bird," I said.

"Just burying a bird, huh?"

"Yeah."

He nodded suspiciously, and I immediately felt like the last time I got pulled over—I think it was for not coming to a complete stop at a red light before turning right. Either that or one of my headlights was out. As a general rule I only ever got pulled over for extremely sad traffic offenses. If I actually did something detrimental or dangerous, I doubt very much that I'd get pulled over. And once I do get pulled over for whatever double yellow line I just crossed, the cops inevitably insist on searching my car for drugs. Every time. The rule seems to be: the sadder the traffic offense, the longer they search. So you'll have to excuse my nerves—they run thin relatively fast when cops are involved. And the funny thing is, I like 'em. Police officers have a sweet cluelessness about them that I've always found endearing, and you can't find that particular cluelessness anywhere else either. They'll stand there, writing you a speeding ticket, and all the while you can see them wishing they were undercover agents about to arrest a drug dealer with one of those pens that is really a machine gun. If that ain't cute, I don't know what is.

"We didn't kill the bird," Jethro said.

The cop raised his eyebrows. "Well, that's what *you* say. I'm afraid we're going to have to run some tests to make sure you're telling the truth."

Jethro's face drained of its color.

"I'm just kidding," the cop said, patting him on the back. "I'm not too worried about that bird. I'm more worried about you kids sitting out here like this. You aren't lost, are you?"

"No, we're staying in town," I said, hoping desperately that there was a town close by that we could be staying in. "We're not from around here. Just driving through."

He nodded again. "You're staying in town, huh?"

"Yep."

"What brings you out here to the dead bird?"

I shrugged my shoulders. "This is a pretty enough landscape to be taking a walk through, isn't it?"

"Well, I grew up here. I'm the wrong person to ask."

"You'll have to take my word for it, then."

He watched us lower the bird into the hole.

"Ain't it a little cold to be taking walks this far out?" he asked.

I shrugged my shoulders. "That depends on if you get cold easily."

We were having one of those conversations that usually only exist in hard-boiled fiction from the forties.

"You kids are staying with your parents?"

"Yep."

"Well, I'd better give you a ride back to town," he said at long last, making his way back to the car. "You finish burying the bird, of course."

I wanted to argue with him, but what was the use? He never would have let us stay out by the side of the road.

"Don't worry," I said to Jethro.

"Why not?"

It was a good question.

"I don't know. Just don't worry."

So there we sat in some Midwestern police car while the whole country was looking for us. Apparently there was no way around introductions, so I introduced us as Miranda and Willard, and he introduced himself as Hank. The three of us got on tolerably well, especially considering that we were playing a very delicate game. Hank had a lot to say. Miranda and Willard mainly just listened. He started off by talking about general things like Alaska and what to do if you get approached by a wild bear. But then he switched to more personal subjects, such as his wife being half Cherokee. Jethro and I were very good at acting nonchalant and nodding. We didn't give each other any looks, and we didn't stumble when we talked. Under the circumstances we did just about as well as could be expected. That doesn't mean, of course, that we were feeling snug in any way. I was ready to throw up. I kept wondering why Hank didn't realize who we were, and then I wondered about how I'd produce a family in whatever town he was taking us to, and then I switched to wondering how Fenton would find us when he turned around to pick us up again. Even if Hank let us out somewhere without demanding to see our family, how would we ever get out of the Midwest again? All my money was in the camper.

When we finally got into town, he asked us where we were staying. I told him I didn't remember the motel name, but I'd recognize it if we passed it. If ever there was thin ice under anyone's feet, it was under ours right then. I pointed to the first motel we saw.

"That's where we're staying."

It was called the Flamingo Motel, and it was only after I had already pointed at it that I realized I probably should have waited for the next one to point at. The Flamingo Motel had a certain melancholic shabbiness about it—you know, the kind that implies that all the housewives and traveling salesmen cheat on their spouses there. I was a little mortified.

"I could be wrong," I said quickly. "I think it was the next one."

His stare burned through my forehead via the rearview mirror.

"Sorry," I said. "I'm bad with remembering places."

After a short pause the game was finally over.

"Miranda, exactly what kind of trouble are you kids in?"

You know that feeling when you're in an elevator and it drops? You know that feeling when you're in a plane to Las Vegas and you fly through an air hole? That feeling you get when you open your front door and find yourself staring at two FBI agents? Well, I felt exactly like that. My heartbeat became a bass drum, and thoughts evaporated in my head like cotton candy.

"What do you mean?" I asked.

I know. It was probably the worst thing I could have said. Innocence can be detrimental when applied wrongly.

But Hank was patient. "I'm trying to help you out. I'm not trying to get you in trouble."

"Thanks."

"You have to understand I can't set you kids off at some motel when I know you're not staying at a motel."

"Sure, I can understand that."

He continued driving. Neither of us said anything for a matter of seconds, and then he glanced back over.

"I'll make a deal with you kids. You tell me the truth, and I get you out of whatever mess you're in."

"We're not in trouble," I said.

"Is it drug related?"

"No."

"Now, look, there are lots of kids your age out there taking drugs. And a lot of them got trapped in that whole life against their will—it happens all the time; but you have to understand that there's always a way out. The earlier, the better."

"Well," I said, "if I were a drug addict I'd certainly feel safe enough to tell you."

I stared vacantly out the window, perhaps even wishing I was back at the prom dancing with George. Life with George would have never come to this. If I'd stayed with him, I'd probably be drinking lattés right now at his parents' ski lodge, and we'd be wearing ugly wooly sweaters and sitting by the fireplace playing Scrabble. Or maybe I actually *would* be doing drugs—together with him—and years later when he'd become governor of Florida, a team of journalists would uncover our youth and the whole country would read about it. Either way, it would never have come to *this*.

We sat on fake leather chairs in the police station, drinking hot chocolate all afternoon. The hot chocolate came in Styrofoam cups and tasted just about as fake as the chairs. But in a way, it felt good sipping warm, brown chemicals under bad lighting. It was nice to be out of the cold. It was nice to be off the side of the road and it was nice to be taken care of so diligently by a police officer who wanted to dig us out of something. My nerves were calmed considerably. Maybe because I knew it was over anyway, and all we had to do now was wait. What better way to meet your doom than with a cup of hot chocolate, steaming into your face?

Jethro liked it too. In fact, he was probably having a ball. His eyes were wide open, his hands tight around the Styrofoam cup, and his thoughts racing the pace of his heart.

"What's going to happen now?" he asked, leaning over and whispering.

"They'll call our parents."

"And then what?"

"Then we go home, Jethro."

"That's *it*?" He sounded disappointed.

"I think so," I said.

"They're not going to lock us up or anything?"

"Doubt it."

"There won't even be a court case?"

"No. There's probably just going to be a private decapitation in the backyard. No big deal."

"Aren't we going to try and escape? We could say we're going to the bathroom and climb through the window!"

"True."

A very slow smile made its way across my face, and I realized that maybe all that was happening was just another form of perfection. Maybe contrary to popular belief, these past two weeks had been a perfect two weeks? Take away any one moment and the whole experience would've been significantly less. I was a girl, so of course I had illusions of Jethro being glued to me forever after—illusions of driving into the sunset with the camper had haunted me. I might not have been dreaming customary dreams, but there was no way around the fact that I was just another naive little teenage dreamer. Sunsets are momentary and every two weeks come to an end. Didn't I know that? And the ending, of course, couldn't have happened anywhere other than a police station in Kansas. It wouldn't have had that well-rounded flavor otherwise.

It was all working out. Maybe not for me, but certainly for Jethro, and that was all that mattered. Honestly. I'm not trying to be righteous, but I can't help but feel a little satisfied when Jethro's eyes glow, even when they're glowing at my nightmare.

Hank came over and sat down next to us. He was wearing a sympathetic face and put his hands on his knees.

"Your mother's on the phone for you, Hester."

"Tell her I'm busy," I said. "Tell her I'm shooting up heroin. She'll like that."

To my surprise he got up and walked back into his office.

"She was very glad to know you were safe," he said when he came back out. "They're taking the next flight out here."

"That's great."

"You'll be all right," he said. "Kids run away all the time."

"I know I might *look* thirteen, but I'm actually eighteen. I don't need to run away from home. I have a legal right to discover that my family is a retardation to my well-being and move out."

He put his hand on my shoulder. "Not with your ten-year-old cousin."

"Hey, she couldn't even kidnap a newt," Jethro said. "I came along by myself."

"I could kidnap a fucking newt! I can't believe you're teaming up with Fenton!"

Outside, the sun was beginning to resign. The wind hadn't stopped sweeping all day, the sky began to let loose, and rain turned the country roads to mud. It was the perfect way for the ax to fall.

"We could find the fuse box, turn off all the lights, and then sneak out," Jethro whispered.

FELL INTO THE OCEAN

I T'S AMAZING how painfully well connected this country is. Its network of ten billion airlines make sure that you can eat peanuts at an altitude of thirty-five thousand feet, while getting from any old cow town to any other old cow town within a matter of hours. The romanticism of long distances has been taken away. Traveling has gotten too fast even for formalities. There's no escaping. Everyone can get their hands on your neck whenever they want to. I've often wondered how things might have turned out had my family been restricted by the vastness of this great country. Who knows? Maybe time would have stepped in and triggered a very different chain of events.

But there was no time. By that same evening, a cab was already pulling up in front of the police station.

Seeing my mother's face again was about as pleasant as having a train drive over my foot. Well, maybe not quite that pleasant.

"Well, I hope you're happy now!" was the first thing she said.

She stood a few feet away from me clutching her handbag and a Kleenex.

"I'm ecstatic," I answered.

"Of course you don't even *realize* what we went through these past two weeks!"

"I have a fair idea," I said. "I saw you all on television. Very touching, Mom."

She turned around and cried out, "I can't put up with this right now. I just can't handle this! After all you just put us through!"

Turning back, she pointed a trembling finger in my face. "There is something very wrong with you, Hester."

And then I was on the plane back to Florida.

Ripping things apart never takes long. Earthquakes demolish cities in a matter of seconds. One bullet can tear through someone's organs and lay a perfectly healthy human specimen flat in a matter of milliseconds. One bomb can do the same to a whole city. A fire can eat a house and burp up a cloud of smoke before the fire engine ever makes it there. Spill water over your computer and all that wonderful machinery dies. It takes forever to cultivate something worthwhile into existence. Why does destruction cost nothing in terms of time?

It was only that morning that I had woken up with my head against Arlene's window. Now it was twelve thirty at night and already the Midwest seemed to be nothing more than mythology. I couldn't even imagine ever having been in Kansas, which was strange considering the plane hadn't even taken off yet. At the same time I couldn't imagine ever having lived in Florida either. Nothing seemed real anymore. I would have murdered for a cigarette. My hands hadn't stopped shaking for three hours now.

Cigarettes being out of the question, I decided to get drunk. I tried to order alcohol on the plane while my mother was in the bathroom, but they wanted to see my ID. I was glaringly underage and didn't have an ID on me, let alone a false one. So, I found myself sitting in perdition armed with nothing but an orange juice.

I never went to jail for kidnapping Jethro. It would have been up to Uncle Norman and Margaret to press charges. However, they declined and nothing legal ever came of it. Uncle Norman didn't give a rat's ass about anything, and Margaret was too religious to send family members to jail. She was too much of a mother. She hated to see things break, she hated to see things spill, and she hated to see things tear. She flinched easily at tragedy, but she was always ready to roll up her sleeves and make the whole world all right again. I was somewhat in awe of her, to tell you the truth. She hadn't cried when she saw Jethro again. She buried him in her arms, looking like she'd won the lottery. It made it obvious that there was no hidden agenda in Margaret Montgomery's universe. I didn't have my doubts about her simplicity. She had wide, empty eyes, and most things she said missed their target by about twenty miles, but her intentions were immaculate. Bleach couldn't have brought about a whiter shade of conscience.

My mother liked to point out impending doom; Margaret liked to pretend it wasn't there. She was the only one who let me believe that maybe we *weren't* standing on the ruins of World War III.

"I hope they straighten you out, honey," she had said as we all sat around at the airport looking grave, preparing to draw the curtain on this uncanny scene.

She meant well by what she said, although it stung. I looked at her and said nothing. Couldn't have said anything if you paid me a million dollars. The moment was just catastrophically void.

Jethro, Margaret, and Uncle Norman were flying back to

Miami. Their flight left half an hour before ours, and I suddenly found myself forced into a farewell with Jethro under a floodlight that washed out all privacy. The moment was so desperate and the future so unthinkable without him that I couldn't even shake hands. There was a lot to say, of course, but none of it could be said there; all that left us with was: "Bye."

As I stared at the ceiling that night, all my thoughts were razor sharp. I cut myself on them and it hurt, but I remained lifeless in my bed with my eyes wide open and dry. Heartbreak must come in a wet as well as dry version. I figured the blood was trickling through my mind, and even though from the outside I looked clean, from the inside I was probably all red.

I understood that there was no sense in living life the way I was before I left. Back then it made sense that I treated everything like a game. It made sense that I laughed and licked my lips when someone insulted me. I could dream up black cynicism like no one else. I could carve expressions into people's faces with what I'd say. Nobody could scathe me. Tragedy was comedy and I watched my life from the first row of the audience. The props were all made out of cardboard, the sky was blue acrylic paint, and the clouds were papier-mâché. I enjoyed watching myself fumble up onstage. I could hold my hand into the fire and laugh, because after all, the flames were only made out of orange fabric.

It made sense that I was immune. I didn't have anything that could be taken away. Everything that I owned didn't mean a goddamn thing to me, and if someone took it away, I'd have shrugged my shoulders. Wasn't real anyway.

I could have spent my whole life like this. But I didn't. One day I went on the road and was sucked into reality. Out there the skies were really blue—blue from the chemical makeup of the

atmosphere. The wind was freezing when it blew over the mead-
ows. Religion was supernatural the way it hung over the Kentucky Sunday—it wasn't something you did so that the neighbors
wouldn't think you were a Satanist, it was something that made
the people out there fall on their knees and get happy.

Food costs money, and the people we met weren't actors.
They said real things, they waited for real answers, and the way
they looked at me made me realize that I was maybe real too. I
wouldn't be surprised if my organs began to work for the first
time. My heart began to pump blood for the first time, my lungs
filled with oxygen for the first time, and my liver cringed at the
toxins I deposited into myself. But more than that, I didn't realize
that I would wake up with emotions every morning.

Ecstasy wasn't a myth anymore, and so neither was the possibility of misery. Of course, I didn't realize that every blow would
leave a bruise now. I never had the sense to play it safe. I didn't
realize just how heavy the value of my life had grown over the
last two weeks. I didn't know that with every day it was becoming
harder to be indifferent—and that soon it would be impossible
altogether. I think maybe there's a law about that: you won't ever
realize a goddamn thing until it's too late.

Now that everything had evaporated and I was back where I
had started from, I found I had acquired an addiction to the way
Jethro's sleepy face would spurt out theories on Martians first
thing in the morning. The way that Fenton couldn't resist laughing sometimes when our arguments became too bizarre. The way
Jesus Freak would explain why he was dragging a cross through
the country as though he were telling us how to use a microwave.
The way that Jack could make me smile at any impending disas-
ters. The way the mornings smelled when you opened the camper

door onto some new scenery. The awkward silences in front of a million coffee machines across the Midwest. Jesus Freak's trail mix assortments. Jethro's drawings. Fenton's notebooks.

I had cravings.

Of course I did. I wasn't really any different from other humans. Once I knew just what it was like having certain luxuries, living without them was like waking up in a nuclear wasteland. Dead streets and bombed buildings all the way to the horizon. It doesn't matter how far you walk, the wind doesn't ever stop sweeping the empty streets, and you never encounter another human being.

GONNA STAND IN RAIN

ONE GOOD thing that came of all this was that I did manage to soil the Day name considerably. People stared. It's a whole different world when you're an outcast. You feel weird doing just about anything. Carry a bloody ax around with you and I guarantee you'll have an easier time of it.

Along with my picture in the local paper came a fascinating story of how I was chemically imbalanced, how I had stumbled into drugs when I was fourteen and kept this habit from my parents all these years. They didn't elaborate on the kinds of drugs I was taking, which I personally found a pity. I think it would have added a lot of spice to go into details. The paper didn't hesitate, however, to mention that I've also been known to deal drugs once in a while. Apparently I married a homeless man (Flaherty) when I turned eighteen, and then brainwashed my ten-year-old cousin. They attributed my marriage to "self-destructive urges." Sure. Some people stick needles in their arm, some people tie a rope around their neck, and others just marry homeless men. Anyway, the story had a good ending: Hester and Jethro were reunited with their families. Jethro was safely back in Miami and Hester had joined a troubled-teen therapy group that meets Thursday nights at the public library. Things were looking up all around.

Not long ago I would have found it fantastic—this story that had been stuck to me with the glue of small-town journalism. I would have walked the streets with my hair gleaming in the sunlight, winking at disturbed passersby, but now I could only sit on my bed, shuddering at the future as I know it will undoubtedly spread out before me.

"It's not so much that I care what people think—at least I fucking hope it's not because I actually care—but people don't *just* think. They'll put their whole life on the back burner just to fry you on the front one. All I want is some peace of mind."

I was watching green television with F in the park. It was a safe place to smoke those days and besides, I loved talking to F about my personalized misery, probably because he never seemed to understand what I was talking about. He listened with enough intensity to power a steam engine, but he never understood what I actually meant. His answers were wonderfully irrelevant and for some reason soothing. We could have coherent conversations on two entirely different subjects and both come out at the other end feeling satisfied.

"Ain't you a little young to be wanting some peace of mind?" he asked, squinting up at me lazily.

"Is that how it goes? There are rules about wanting some peace of mind?"

"*I'm* old enough for it, but I don't know about you. You should be wanting to sink your teeth into something."

"Well, I won't talk for all people my age," I said. "I'll just talk for myself. And I'm ready to retire."

"Hmm."

"Sometimes I wish that Aunt Margaret would have pressed charges. It would be great to have bars between me and my family."

"They have visiting hours in jails."

"I'm just being a hopeless romantic."

We abandoned our dialogue for a few minutes to watch a beer commercial.

"Hey, whatever happened to that kid who came running out here asking you to marry him a few months back?" F asked absentmindedly.

I could never think about Fenton without stumbling over awkward thoughts now.

"We lost track of each other in Kansas. Couldn't tell you where he is."

"Ah. Kansas. Boy, I never saw so many religious nutcases in one place. I don't travel anymore, but back in the day I traveled through the Bible Belt quite a bit, and I'll tell you, I couldn't even take a *piss* without looking over my shoulder—what with all the goddamn billboards warning you about Jesus and whatnot watching your every move."

My thoughts were drowning somewhere in a sea of blackstrap molasses. It can hurt when you smile at the wrong time, but there's something nice about defying logic.

"Well, I better get going. I'm supposed to meet with a bunch of troubled teens up in the library. I'm already late."

"Who'd want to meet with a bunch of troubled teens?" he asked, confused.

"I think there's only about two people there of their own free will, and they're obviously not right in the head."

It was true. There was this obese girl called Emily who signed herself up so that she could talk about her weight issues every week and make a whole bunch of strangers sit through the goddamn ordeal. As though life wasn't shitty enough. The other one was this kid called Bob. Bob was just bored. He got a kick out of listening to fucked-up, real-life stories.

"You're late, Hester," Mrs. Lyall said.

Mrs. Lyall was the lady who ran the meetings. Fresh out of school with a degree in psychology. She must have been in her late twenties; kinda ugly, but I could see her getting a lot of attention from men if she just threw on a short red dress. She was round in the face and had circles under her eyes, but she had a decent body and well-shaped lips. She was never quite as acidic in her actions as she was in her looks.

"You missed a lot, I'm afraid," she said, gesturing to an empty chair.

"Sorry. There was a car crash. I had to give mouth-to-mouth while the ambulance arrived."

Mrs. Lyall looked at me as though she hadn't slept in a decade. "Hester, we're all friends here. We can say anything we want in this room, as long as it's the truth."

"I know."

"Okay?"

"Okay."

She had the habit of randomly depositing "okay" into silences.

"We're here to open up to each other. That's why we meet here every Thursday—to find out that we're not alone, we're not overlooked, and there are people who *will* listen and understand and lend a hand. We want to feel lighter when we walk out of here, right?"

A general murmur of grudging agreement traveled through the room.

"Peter, you were in the middle of telling us about this girl that you like. Why don't you finish now that we're all here?"

Peter looked about ready to die. I didn't blame him. Talk about hell walking around on earth!

Mrs. Lyall stretched a tired smile across her face and folded her hands attentively. "Go on."

"Well," he said eventually, keeping his eyes close to the vicinity of his right pant leg, "she just ignores me."

"Did you ever talk to her?"

"Yeah, I asked her out this one time. She just laughed. She was with all her friends and just laughed."

Mrs. Lyall nodded him on. "And how did that make you feel, Peter?"

"Embarrassed. Just like I don't think anything is worth it anymore. I thought about killing myself last week."

I couldn't help but let out a short laugh. It was completely tasteless, and I had not intended it.

"Yes?" Mrs. Lyall asked, turning toward me.

"I'm sorry," I said.

"Is there something you want to share with Peter?"

Peter was barely seventeen. His acne was in full bloom and his features were still settling in. He glanced at me quickly and then lodged his stare back at his pant leg. You don't joke around with kids this age. They're just about the most fragile form of a human entity. Say something weird about the shape of their nose or a song they like and you've planted a crater in their life.

"I'm sorry," I said, trying not to burst out again, "but I really don't see how I qualify to open my mouth."

"I'm sure you can relate to Peter's problem in some way. We all learn from each other."

I thought for a second.

"Well, look, there's this saying," I began. "'If you can't be with the one you love, keep lovin' someone else.' You might wanna note that down somewhere, Peter."

Mrs. Lyall frowned. "How exactly does that quote apply to Peter's case?"

"Depends on how Peter wants to bend it around. Personally, I think it's kind of obvious. He thinks this mediocre pile of shit he has a crush on is the meaning of his life, and he better kill himself over her bad manners—well, I'd say it's time for him to be interested in a life-form that isn't a mediocre pile of shit. I don't know if you've noticed, Peter, but there's a hell of a variety out there, and some girls are actually decent."

"Excuse me," Emily broke in, "I just want to say that it's not really fair to call someone you never met a 'mediocre pile of shit.' That's a really strong expression."

"So? You want me to find a weaker expression?"

"No, I just think it's disrespectful to that girl. You don't know what goes on in her life. You don't know her side of the story."

I rolled my eyes. "I'm obviously just making a point here, not writing someone's fucking biography. If you wanna research her life's history, then why don't you do that?"

"All I'm saying is people shouldn't talk about other people like that until you know them," Emily went right on. "People always call me names, just because of what I look like, and that really hurts, you know. People should take the time to get to know someone. It's not my fault that I look like this, you know.

I was born with these genes, and all I want is to have the chances everyone else gets."

"Who's talking about you here?" I asked. "Did any of us call you a blimp?"

I was convinced Emily was an evil species of fungus—something that only breeds in certain midsized Floridian towns on the Gulf of Mexico. There she sat, happy as a clam, feeding off of our misery. She just sat there, and no matter what subject was under discussion, she'd barge in from some dark corner and lay her weight problem all over the table. She didn't just lay it on the table, she forced it down everyone's throats until it came up and out our ears—all with that innocent, plaintive voice of hers, and her insipid eyes stuck in an ocean of a face.

"I'm just expressing what I feel," she said. "And I feel that as obese children we're always the target of everyone else. We're never looked at for who we are, just what we look like."

"What the hell's wrong with you? You really think everyone's agenda is built around your physique?" I asked.

She looked a little lost. "Well, I just think—"

I cut her off. "So maybe some kids like to pick on other kids. What else is new? I don't know what planet you think we're on—but this is Earth, we had the Inquisition and the Holocaust here. I wouldn't waste time wondering why kids pick on you. I'd wonder why the hell you love it so much. If you really had a problem about the fact that you weigh two tons, you'd have signed up at the gym rather than here. Your fat ass wouldn't be planted on that plastic chair over there. It would be on the treadmill. But you love it. You love the fact that you can sit there every Thursday and drown us out."

"Okay, I think that's enough for now, Hester," Mrs. Lyall broke in sharply. She was feeling nervous. I guess maybe her psychology degree wasn't quite as bulletproof as she had anticipated. The breath she took came out in a little shiver. She placed the clipboard on her lap and looked around the room for a change of subject.

"Russell, how is it going with that addiction this week?"

And that's how it went all afternoon. I swear to God I was almost looking forward to seeing my mom again—until I remembered that she was the one who'd gotten me into this in the first place. The day was pushing toward early evening, and I found myself fumbling for a cigarette out on the parking lot curb. You know when you put a white sock in the wash with a bunch of bright green sweaters? Well, I felt a little like that white sock probably feels. Discolored, deflated, and raw. My nerves felt exposed, and every sweep of the humid breeze scraped hard against them.

"Hester, right?"

I looked up and there stood Ronald Peterson.

"We graduated together," he continued with a broad grin that threatened to dive off his face at both ends. "Ronald Peterson. Remember me?"

"That's right," I said. "Ronald Peterson."

"They gave me your high school diploma at graduation," he said.

"Well, I figured as much," I said. "I have yours, and if you ask me, that was the saving grace of all those years in school."

"Yeah, really," he said. "Hey, I read about you in the paper."

"Oh, I read about that too."

"That's fucking awesome!"

"The part about my drug dealing or the part about the kidnapping?"

"Come on, Hester! We're barely out of school for half a year and you've already made it onto national television. Do you even realize how amazing that is?"

Ronald was one of those eager-looking guys who are always acting like they're about to take aim and blow a deer off the face of the earth. He started conversations just because he liked to hear himself talk. Frankly, I would have preferred discussing my kidnapping skills with a cucumber, but I guess in the absence of a cucumber one will settle for less.

"Hey, you wanna come to this party tonight?" he asked.

My mom's car pulled up in front of us just then. She had a large Yale sticker on the back window. No one we were even remotely related to had gone to Yale, but I guess it boosted her confidence when she parallel parked.

"Yeah, I'd like to come," I said.

FOOL GOT HAPPY

MY MOTHER and I didn't talk all too much. Not that we ever had, but since my return our conversations had begun to resemble scenes from some avant-garde theater piece where it is strictly prohibited for anything to actually make sense. I'd go so far as to say that we interacted on an amoebic level.

"Well?" she asked, making a sharp right out of the parking lot.

"Well, what?"

"Well, how was it? Are you progressing?"

"Sure."

She sighed. "Hester, I really can't handle this attitude of yours anymore."

"What attitude? I said I was progressing, didn't I?"

"That's exactly what I mean. You're obviously *lying*."

"Well, yeah."

"What do you mean 'well, yeah'?"

"Come on, there are just certain truths you know you'd have no use for. We'd just argue."

She threw her hands up in the air with despondency. "Oh my God, that's what I'm always talking about—you treat me like some imbecile who needs everything watered down!"

"I was being polite."

"Polite my ass. No one in this family treats me like a human being anymore. Who am I kidding? I shouldn't even bother anymore."

"Jesus Christ, Mom."

"Why don't you send me off to an old people's home right away and be rid of me?"

Life seemed to have become one never-ending psychological thriller.

"Okay, fine," I said. "You asked me did I make any progress? No, I didn't. I'd have made more progress gluing my thigh to a palm tree and reciting the Constitution backwards."

She glanced over quickly and then stared back at the road silently.

"Oh, and another thing: Mrs. Lyall thinks I have trouble controlling my rage. So I'm not just *not* making progress, I'm actually going backwards."

My mom seemed very placid all of a sudden. "Now, Hester, you're just working through things. That's the way it goes. You're not going to get anywhere if you don't work through things."

"I'm not working through anything. I'm listening to a bunch of kids complaining and feeling sorry for their lame bullshit lives. There are reality TV shows that cover that very thoroughly. I don't see why I have to drive to the library every week to witness it in three dimensions."

"Because you *need* this interaction, Hester."

"Like I need a nose transplant maybe."

"Honey, come on now. Stop acting like you're in third grade. This is for your own good. I'm trying to help you out of this situation you managed to get yourself into, and just for your information: you still have a good chance. You can still get into college, maybe a year late, but it's still possible."

"Great."

"If you'd just let all this bitterness out of your system and open yourself up to the world, you'd be surprised where you could get."

I looked over at her. "I was feeling kinda cozy in that 'situation' I managed to get myself into."

"Oh, taking someone's child away from them without a word is what you call cozy?"

"Best thing I ever did."

I didn't see any particular advantage in clarifying things further.

"Well, in any case, we made a deal, young lady, and we're going to stick to it."

(The deal was: if I managed to straighten out and get accepted into college, I was allowed to have contact with Jethro again.)

"Yeah, I know we made a deal. Trust me, I know."

I hated my mother so much that I began not to hate her at all. What was the point? I might as well sit down and hate a brick wall. Was I really going to involve her in meaningful thoughts? Talking of which, I hadn't had a meaningful thought for an awful long time. My apathy had grown so thick that I couldn't lift my little finger. My mother moved me around like a pawn. I didn't much cooperate, but I didn't have the energy to stem my feet up against it either. I used to put so much work and thought into evading my family—the way I worked against their mediocre little plans and lonely dreams for me was an art form. I must have liked coming up with elaborate plans to jump aside. I must have been glad for all of them in some twisted way; I always believed I was a masochist anyway.

But now my family's existence had lost its significance. I had probably matured and learned the sad truth about just how vastly bland my games had been previous to the trip through the Midwest. Maybe that's why I said yes to a party that Ron Peterson was offering up. Ronald Peterson of all people. What was I thinking? I began to wonder whether I really *was* suffering from psychological mishaps.

I can't remember much more than wandering into a crowded house and making straight for a dining table, cluttered with bottles. Bottles that had every shape and color you could wish or dream for. I'd never been fond of alcohol, and my taste buds had never agreed with the rest of the world on the flavors being anything other than rubbing alcohol. However, that night it all looked like candy to me, and I wondered why I hadn't thought of getting wasted earlier. I scanned over the table quickly and then made for the vodka. I remember filling up a white plastic cup.

I turned, leaned myself against the table, and took in my environment. The rooms were dark and filled with those typical white sofas and lampshades that rich people always think they need if they live by the beach. The music came drifting through the smoke and consisted mainly of hip-hop. There was a door that opened up to an outside area with a pool. There was beer already seeping into the carpet and a glass flamingo was lying shattered next to the mantelpiece. Some kid's parents were going to have a very banal return from their romantic weekend.

I refilled the plastic cup and had a short conversation with someone called Bart about my marriage.

"It's not that bad, Bart. Really. You just gotta find that one person you'd never marry in a million years, and marry that person. Nothing can go wrong, 'cause you're starting backwards. You start off hating each other, and it can't get worse than that—just a whole lot better."

"Whatever. I'm never getting married—I mean not until I'm like thirty-five or something."

"Yeah, well, no one here's tryin' to write you up a marriage license, so you can breathe easy, buddy. I'm just telling you the way to do it *when* you do it."

"If everything's so great then where's your husband?"

"He isn't here, and that's what's so great about it. We just lose track of each other. Just like that. Happens all the time."

"You're fucked up."

"Why, look who's talking."

"Hey, everything that *I* do, nobody knows about. Everything *you* do ends up in the papers."

"Take it easy. I'm just kidding, Bart. God! Anyway, some people, like Ron Peterson, actually think that's an achievement."

I'm sure it all got more interesting after that, but I can't remember. The sad part is, I might have had a ball. Who knows? Maybe it was all worth it, and I don't have a clue. I really wouldn't be surprised. Wouldn't be surprised at all if the best night of my life was a night erased from memory and replaced by solid black.

Anyway, I did end up facedown in our neighbor's bushes the following morning. Incidentally, I also discovered that day that a hangover has the power to make you think more suicidal thoughts in any given minute than most other catastrophic occasions. Pain has a cute way of driving all sorry bullshit straight out of your head and replacing it with an immediacy for which you are willing to do anything. The good thing about hangovers is of course that you have no energy left over to feel embarrassed. That right there might be the only reason we survive these kinds of days at all. I can't imagine living through all that pain and having to be conscious of your tailor-made mortification at the same time. That's not to say that it's impossible to feel embarrassed, because it's probably the easiest emotion to indulge in, but I'm just saying if the grade of your hangover is such that death seems a gift from heaven, then you don't bother much with minor details.

"Oh my Lord! Is that you, Hester? Hester Day?"

I became aware of my entire body with that exclamation. It's very strange when in a matter of a single second you go from a certified nothingness to the proud owner of a whole biodegradable, humanoid body. Life flushing into you from near death feels a little like a tornado. And opening my eyes proved to be about as hard as that time when I was fresh out of the hot womb, blinking at the lights of a hospital ceiling. The sun poured into my burning sockets like chloride. It took a few seconds, but eventually Mrs. Wilkinson's face swam into view in the overexposed day. Mrs. Wilkinson was our neighbor to the right.

"Are—are you all right down there?"

I tried to turn over but found myself to be a little on the paralyzed side.

"What's wrong?"

She began to look worried when I didn't answer her.

"Good God, what's *wrong*?"

It looked like she was going to break down any minute, so I

made the effort to pull myself up in one fast motion. Boy, did I wish I would have fallen into our other neighbor's bushes. He wouldn't have minded at all—I hardly ever saw him without a glass of whiskey in his hands. My mother had had numerable talks with him about advertising alcohol so blatantly in front of her children.

"I'm sorry about your plant, Mrs. Wilkinson," I faltered.

"What happened?"

"I got plastered last night, unexpectedly of course, and woke up here."

She stared at me wide-eyed. "Is that vomit?"

"Yeah. I wouldn't worry too much, it'll probably just fertilize the bush anyway."

"It will?"

"I'm pretty sure, yeah."

I was standing on my own two feet by that time. Mrs. Wilkinson and I stared at each other a silent while longer, and then I sighed and ran my hand over my forehead.

"Anyway, I have to go now," I said. "Have a good one."

My body begged to be dead. I could feel my organs turning green inside of me, shriveling into disgusted little masses of meat. I remember standing in our driveway, swaying and staring at the house. Who knows how long I stood there—it might have taken me about an hour just contemplating the horrors of entering that house, stumbling through those rooms, through all that shrapnel and contempt. They'll demand to know why I got drunk, what I drank, how many STD-infested men I slept with, what I shot up my veins, and all that. How would I answer them? I'd obviously be the last to know the answers to any of those questions.

I ended up standing there long enough for my dad to appear in the front door with his weekend clothes on.

"Hey there," he said, stopping in front of me, squinting into the sunlight with his golf equipment slung over his back. "You look like shit, honey."

"That's kind of what I feel like too."

"Well, whatever happened, I'm not interested. You're going to have to realize one of these days that there are consequences to actions."

I couldn't care less just then.

"Oh, one more thing, Hester," he said after a pause. "I'd appreciate it if you wouldn't give your mother any more reasons to have nervous breakdowns."

I gave him as best of a dark look as I could through my alcohol poisoning.

"I *mean* it," he said. "Every time she throws a fit, *I'm* the one who has to deal with it."

"Well, I'm sure that sucks, and if I ever start *giving* a shit, I'll let you know right away."

That's what I *thought*.

What I said was: "I'll do what I can."

I didn't really see why my dad had a right to complain about his wife to me. *He* was the man who willingly signed a marriage contract with her. No one held a gun to his head—he did it of his own free will. And now we were all supposed to feel sorry because he had to talk to her every night?

I stood on the front lawn a while longer after he'd pulled out of the driveway, probably because the thought of mounting the front steps seemed as far off as the Himalayas. I took a step, swayed a little, and then everything began to turn brown around the edges. The bleached day began to be eaten away. The brown inched farther and farther into the picture, until at last everything was black. I thought I could hear myself topple over.

By the time I woke up, it was the afternoon. I was lying in a hospital bed and was attached to a bottle that dangled somewhere above me. The room was very white and small. It was empty except for a picture of a sailboat and for my sister, who sat next to the bed reading a magazine. She turned her head and glanced expressionlessly at me.

"They pumped your stomach," she said dryly.

DON'T YOU LET IT FALL

IT TURNED out to be a long day. I didn't stop feeling like shit until about one in the morning, and until then the hours were filled with many pleasurable moments. To begin with there was my sister, who wouldn't stop flipping through magazines at my bedside like she was machine-gunning down enemy troops. She'd intersperse random comments and questions that tore through every angle of my hot head.

"What the hell's up with you kidnapping Jethro anyway?"

"He came on his own account."

And not much later:

"I don't understand how you could have married that homeless guy, Fenton."

"That's all right."

"Did you guys have sex?"

"Yes."

Lies are sometimes irresistible.

I stared up at the yellow fluid suspended over my head with a vast blank spreading through my mind to some distant horizon. Learning your stomach has just been pumped doesn't always leave you with much to say. The room felt sterile, empty, and kind of massive, despite how small it actually was.

"Aren't you supposed to be in Arizona or something?" I asked eventually.

"It's a long weekend."

"Oh."

Well, after a few hard-earned seconds I turned toward her again. "Don't you have anything better to do on a long weekend?"

She looked about ready to skin me alive. "Do you honestly think I volunteered to sit here?"

"No."

My eyes wandered down the rubber tube all the way to my hand, where a thick square bandage hid the particulars of how the liquid from the tube was being deposited into my body.

"Is that a *needle* in my hand?"

"It's about two inches long. I saw them put it in."

I closed my eyes and slowly took a few heavy breaths. I had a hard time with needles. The last thing I needed to know right then were the specifics of the two-inch needle in my hand.

"The whole thing was completely unnecessary too," Hannah continued. "The doctor said you fainted from dehydration, but Mom insisted they pump your stomach anyway. She said you probably mixed drugs with alcohol and if they didn't pump your stomach, she'd sue the hospital."

I opened my eyes slowly.

"I guess every soap opera has its hospital scene."

"That's not funny, Hester."

"You're telling *me* that?"

Hannah put her magazine down and stared at me with real emotion.

"I hate you, Hester," she said.

She might as well have explained to me that grass is usually green or that fish need water to survive.

"I know," I replied.

"No you *don't*. This is not just stupid sibling shit, this is *real*. I really do hate you."

I still didn't see how any of this was news.

"No, trust me, I really know."

"Look," she said, "I'm sick and tired of everything revolving around *you*! I have a life too. This is a long weekend off from school. *I* should be getting drunk. *I* should be waking up in the neighbor's bushes, not you. And instead, I'm sitting here in a fucking hospital, because you just can't get enough of it!"

"Enough of 'it'?"

"Drama! You just wallow in it. You'll do anything for it."

I tilted my head in the manner that dogs do when they believe humans will make more sense if viewed at an angle. Drama?

"*Drama?*"

"You obviously can't live without it."

"Hold it—hold it right there. Are you saying I *want* this? I wanted to be in the paper, I want to be in the hospital with a fucking needle in my hand?"

"Oh please. Suddenly you have scruples?"

"What?"

This was making no sense. I really tried to understand, but nothing fell into place. Suddenly I was an attention-craving drama queen and my sister was the silent sufferer? The good kid who always got left behind? Either the nurses had put something in that liquid that was dripping into my bloodstream, or it was in Hannah's blood that these things were swimming. In any case, one of us was stark raving mad, and I preferred it not be me.

"Look, can we take a rain check on this conversation?" I asked. "I feel sick."

"What do *I* care if you're sick? I'm stuck here having to *watch* you be sick. And if I'm stuck here, I might as well let you know what a selfish bitch you are. You have no right to fuck up my life just because you love being the center of attention. And I'm warning you, Hester, this better be the last time, because next time, things will be very different."

She stopped there. Obviously she hadn't prepared a sample of the consequences to her threat and so left us dangling somewhere, waiting.

I really didn't know how to respond to any of her comments. It's like when you have to move a piano up a narrow staircase and you can't even decide where to grab hold of the damn thing. Truth be told, I hadn't thought of my sister in so long that her sudden existence right next to me seemed a little unwieldy and ethereal. And the fact that she looked so distraught because *she* wasn't the one lying drunk in the bushes didn't make the situation any less weird. Her skin wasn't doing too well and her hair was haloed by the sun skimming through the blinds. I remembered all my laborious hatred for her—somewhere, seemingly years ago, before I left home. Her features were heavy, and you could see the emotions digging through her guts, just like I had often felt them in myself.

"You and Mom are such a pain in the ass," she muttered, throwing her magazine down and picking up a new one.

"*Me and Mom?*" I gasped. "I hate to sound weird about this, but I always thought it was *you* and Mom that were the pain in the ass."

"Well, it's *not*, okay? It's *you* and Mom."

Uncomfortable pause.

"How do you know for sure, though?" I asked, confused.

"*Fuck you.* That's how I know."

"How's that an answer? I'm serious about this."

She looked at me a little weird, maybe because I did indeed seem distressed about the news that I was a drama queen.

"Don't you know what a pain in the ass is? It's a pain—right here." She pointed to her ass. "And that's what you are. A pain in the ass."

I wanted to harpoon her for being such a retarded conversationalist. Not only for that, of course. She was also a waste of space and an egotistical piece of shit, and she must have been sharing that brain cell with God knows how many other whitetrash radicals. But the longer I looked at her the more I realized I wasn't even looking for the harpoon. I was looking for the *desire* to dig it into her. And it just wasn't there.

Something began to well up in my eyes, and when I blinked, two fat streams of tears rolled down my cheeks like worms. They felt warm, and I felt embarrassed to the bottom of my stomach. But there wasn't anything I could do. The worms dripped off my chin and soaked into the sheets, and the whole scene passed without me having any say in the matter. I had to watch helplessly as my body was overtaken by emotions that I'd only known from school plays, where ambitious actors overcompensated for their drab Floridian lives.

"*Now what?*" Hannah asked, visibly thrown off. In fact, she looked a little like I had just morphed into a caribou.

I returned the look. "I really couldn't tell you."

After which we shared the most awkward silence that has ever been shared in the history of awkward silences. The magazine crinkled under the weight of her right thumb and the muffled sounds of hospital noises crawled through the walls. I pretended to be interested in the sailboat picture, but the warm tears just kept on rolling down and soaking into the sheets. Something deep was obviously going on, and most likely it would pass us both by and we'd never know just how profound that moment actually was. We did have a conversation, but it was so bizarre that I don't know to this day what the hell it was all about. And yet, at the time it made perfect sense.

I looked up and found Hannah's face still disturbed.

"*What?*" I said. I tried to sound unaffected, but that's never easy when your eyes are bloodshot and glossy and you're connected to a bottle dangling over your head.

"What do you mean 'what'?" she asked. "*You* what?"

I tried to wipe the water off my face.

"I was happy," I said. "Just me and Jethro, Duncan, and that fucking jerk . . ."

Her mouth dropped open. "Are you talking about the homeless guy?"

I nodded. "He's not really all that homeless."

"Whatever, I don't even know if I want to have this conversation."

"Every day there was some new reason to jump over fences in the middle of the night," I continued all the same. "It was going good. Better than ever. And now I'm here. Why am I back here? What do I care if you hate me if I can't be bothered to hate you back?"

"Uh, okay . . ."

"Anyway, what's in it for you, Hannah? Don't you ever get bored being so religiously against me?"

I looked at her for an answer, but she came up with nothing.

"You probably knew me once at some point, but you don't really know anything anymore. I have other things I think about these days. Did you ever feel like you were older and younger at the same time? I mean like sixty and four years old all at once? It's hard to explain."

Hannah stared. "This is getting *weird.*"

"You're telling *me* that?" I said, applying my arm to my eyes. "I didn't even know I was born with a faucet to turn on."

Hannah got up. She seemed a little shaken.

"I'm going to go to the bathroom."

"Okay."

I looked after her, feeling incredibly sober. Had we made peace? I'd probably never know. When she came back, she went on reading her magazine and I pretended to sleep.

When my parents got back, things didn't get any better.

"*You could have died!*"

The thing my mom didn't understand was that practically everyone could have died at any given moment of the day. Saying "you could have died" was just about the most universal thing to say. Planes could crash. Doctors could fuck up heart transplants. Clumsy teenage suicides could have worked out. I didn't bother telling my mom this, though. Words seemed to be made of lead, and no matter what way the traffic went, it hurt, crawling through my soft insides. I was satisfied with simply watching my mother's lips move and her hands fly through the air in erratic explanations.

My dad stood around near the window and looked at his wristwatch a lot. The one thing I had in common with my dad was that most of the time we were always wishing we were somewhere else.

"Are you listening to me?" my mom said after a good while. "Do you have any idea how dangerous it is to mix drugs with alcohol? We could be burying you right this minute!"

"I doubt you'd be burying me right this minute if I only died a few hours ago."

I said it for lack of something more impressive to say.

"Isn't that just like you?" she exclaimed. "I'm talking about your *life* here. Your *life*, Hester!"

That's how it went all day long until they left me alone and it was dark outside. The lights in the room were finally out, the noise was gone, and everything was black. I closed my eyes and tried to sleep or wait until my head felt a little less like a cast-iron monument. The silence became hypnotizing and although the nausea and the tube attached to my hand didn't exactly rock me right to sleep, my body was exhausted enough to fall into some bottomless hole. And not much later I was flying through the Midwest in a car. Fenton was at the wheel and Jethro sat beside him, suggesting we fly to Spain. I sat by the window with my feet on the dashboard, like I'd spent so many of our earlier days on the road. The clouds passed us by, and we could see the fields, the Mississippi River, the Everglades, the bright blue Caribbean. Don't ask me what route we were taking to Spain, but it was a great route. In fact, it was the best time I'd ever had in a car.

Waking up to a dark hospital scene let my spirits crash through the floor into the core of the earth. The pain in my head was gone, but loneliness had never felt so devastating before. Not even that first night, when I realized I was back home and the loss of everything that mattered was still fresh and wet. All this while I had survived on the hope that with time things wouldn't matter as much. Isn't there a rumor that time erodes feelings? Well either that rumor isn't true, or I had no patience to wait long enough, because now that physical pain was over I decided I'd rather live in eternal alcohol poisoning if it would just preoccupy me and keep me from being homesick. I probably called it "homesick" because I was too scared to say "love".

I thought of Jethro's hand lying on a piece of scrap paper, tracing out spacemen with names like Daring Dan and Black Griffin. All those mornings spent drinking coffee at roadside diners. Fuel pumps. Lots of drawings. Hillbillies. Philosophy. I'd forgotten how much Fenton and I would tear the world apart. We sure could keep a conversation going long past its bedtime.

I suddenly saw my life clearly in perspective, as though it were on a screen—more than a screen, I saw it in three dimensions—every aspect of it blown to crystal-clear proportions. Every conceivable flaw was magnified to fantastic size.

I sat up in bed and pulled the bandage slowly off my hand. I felt for the needle, closed my eyes hard, and pulled it out. To this day I believe that pulling that needle out of my own hand was one of the hardest feats I have ever performed. Disconnected from the bottle, I pushed the blankets back and began to search the room for my clothes. I didn't know what I was planning to do, but I knew I had to get out of that bed, and I knew I wasn't going anywhere in that white hospital gown. I found a sweater and some skirt of mine folded in the corner on a chair and quickly struggled my way into them. I wiped my hand frantically over my cheeks to try and remove all visible tear tracks, and then I kicked the door open carefully.

The walls were painted pale green out in the hallway and things smelled of rubbing alcohol. The lighting drowned everyone in a universe of hypodermic needles and cotton balls. It made me a little weak in the knees to think that behind all these walls human bodies were being treated like the unsuspecting meat you find lying around in butcher shops. I walked down various hallways, took a few elevator stops down, and judging by the amount of people being pushed around on gurneys, I soon found myself in the emergency ward. I think I was trying to find the canteen initially. Someplace where the existence of coffee was a reality. Meanwhile, people were being pushed past me with arms drowned in blood, wads of cotton sloppily attached over their eyes, or third-degree burns spread over their chests. Some of them were delirious, others were screaming out words that the nurses ignored with hospital talk. The lucky ones had passed out long ago. It was a little intimidating, and I inched along the walls feeling like an intruder. Farther down the hall was a small waiting room with a gray carpet and old seats occupied by a tired-looking congregation of invalids and family members. There was a vending machine squeezed into the corner and some medical magazines on a table. I wondered who in their right mind would ever leaf through a medical magazine.

Walking on, I found another elevator. I pressed the button and stared intently at the metal doors so that I wouldn't have to start some lame conversation with the figure that had just shuffled up behind me. Making small talk with hospital strangers at three in the morning wasn't appealing right then.

Inside the elevator we pressed ourselves into opposite corners, and only after the doors had closed did I glance up quickly. And then I realized in brilliant slow motion that the man standing opposite me with the bandage pulled across the middle of his face, looking like a sour Civil War victim, was Fenton Flaherty.

My stomach dropped to somewhere down south. All my carefully erected certainties were out the window, the floor was suddenly pulled from beneath my feet, and all around me was deep space.

THEY DON'T MAKE 'EM LIKE YOU ANYMORE

IT'S ABSURD how time can change absolutely nothing if you won't let it. Fenton stood under the elevator lamp looking no different from the day that we fought about burying the bird—in fact, I wouldn't be surprised if there were still traces of that argument left in his skin. The light crept into his face and let the shadows under his eyes leak into black puddles. I could only really see his eyes and mouth, since the middle of his face was bandaged up horizontally, and that woolly Swiss Alps hat was pulled down over his hair.

We ended up in some kind of quiet stupor that dragged minutes into centuries, frozen against opposite walls as though we had caught each other red-handed in the middle of signing our souls over to the devil. The elevator was moving upward for longer than the building could possibly have provided floors for. It didn't matter much. I was more preoccupied with the serenity that shock could provide than with the logistics of time and space. I wanted to say something, but found that the correct word to begin with wasn't part of the English language—or any language for that matter. I wanted to feel something, but every feeling threatened to be ludicrous. From the outside we must have looked almost disinterested in the meeting.

The elevator stopped abruptly on the third floor. Neither of us moved. The door slid open to reveal a long, empty hallway and then closed again.

"Hester, what the hell are you doing here?"

The way that Fenton asked it, you'd think I'd wandered into his private home while he was taking a bath and that we'd never met before. I felt comfortable right away.

"I had a hangover."

"Who goes to the hospital for a hangover?"

"Believe me, I didn't drive *myself* here. I would have been happier staying in the bush I woke up in."

"What bush?"

"Our neighbor's. I don't know how I got there either, incidentally."

"I thought you didn't even like alcohol."

"I don't."

"So why are you acting like you're part of some fucking fraternity?"

"It's a long story."

"So?"

"Let's skip it, okay? It's not a good story."

"You're right; maybe I don't want to know."

We stared each other down.

"What's *your* excuse for being here?" I asked.

"My nose broke."

"On its own?"

"With the help of Jesus Freak's cross. I was trying to get to some manuscripts behind it and it slipped and hit me in the face."

"Aren't you supposed to be in Kansas?" I asked.

"Why should I be in Kansas?"

"I don't know. Why should you be back *here*?"

"There aren't any places I should or shouldn't be at," he said.

I pushed the button for the ground floor.

"I used to think of you as some hyperpretentious, intellectual idiot," I said, leaning against the wall next to him. "But, hey, it was Florida and it was summer, and it wasn't exactly like there were a whole bunch of beatnik wannabes nesting out in the library. Arguing with you about things that didn't matter sure beat the hell out of doing just about anything else."

"Are you trying to be endearing?" Fenton asked.

"Actually, I'm trying very hard *not* to be endearing."

"For any particular reason?"

I took a deep breath. "I'm glad to see you, Fenton."

I had originally intended to look him straight in the eyes when I said this but I just couldn't do it. It wasn't easy, folks. And it sounded awful too.

"I don't even care *why* you came back here," I continued. "You could have come back here to go buy a lawn mower for all I care. I'm just so fucking glad to see you that I think it might be unhealthy. And I'm afraid there's no nice way to put it."

He still didn't say anything. I was on the verge of believing that I had deeply embarrassed him, or maybe just myself. So I fell back on an old habit that's never left me since kindergarten. I closed my eyes. It's a wonderfully pointless technique of self-defense when the water runs high.

But then I felt his hand crawl over my hair.

"You're breaking the random-body-part rule," I said.

EPILOGUE
(THIS IS HOW IT GOES)

HEY, MOM?"

I was holding the receiver of a pay phone in my hand under the nasty lights of a gas station. Fenton was fueling up the camper.

"Yes?" My mother's voice sounded like it was walking a tight-rope.

"It's Hester."

Her voice broke. Hysterics spilled from the cracks. "Hester, where are you? Where are you calling from? Why aren't you in your bed? What time is it?"

"It's about four thirty a.m."

"Where the *hell* are you?"

"At a gas station."

Deep breath. I could see her lip twitching and her thoughts racing, trying to hit on something to say. Finally, her voice came again.

"This had better be some kind of very tasteless joke, young lady."

"It's not," I said. "I just wanted to call and let you know that I wasn't at the hospital anymore. It would save you the trip in the morning, and besides, I figured I'd say good-bye this time."

"This time? What are you talking about? Why did you leave the hospital?"

"Why?" I smiled despite myself. "Come on, Mom . . ."

My voice trailed off and I didn't bother finishing. The silence on the other end was more loaded than any dialogue we had ever shared before. Maybe even monumental. It was almost as though there was no need to continue talking, and all that could ever be said had been said—with etiquette and all the goodwill you could ask for. Quite frankly, it made my hair stand on end. That which years and years of floundering about had never accomplished was done with half a sentence. An amputee. And there was my mother, standing on the other side of a phone line, with a clear visual of me. She already knew everything that I was planning to say, or not to say.

"Where are you, Hester?" she said.

I could hear a dry swallow of horror on the other end.

"At a gas station."

"Hester, *where are you?* What gas station? I'm picking you up."

"We both know you won't see me again."

I said it honestly. I said it with all the graces I had never had. No humor, no sarcasm, no flavoring—just a lonely fact, presented with all the love that I could possibly muster. It was the cleanest thing I had ever said to a parent.

My mother's machinery creaked under the stress. Smoke began to appear between the cogwheels.

"I'm picking you up right now, Hester," she stammered. "I'm not going to play this little game of yours!"

"That's all right," I said. "I don't think it would be a good idea for you to play this game with me anyway."

"Stop it."

"Stop what? You know I'm not doing anything."

"Oh, you're *not*? Then what's this phone call all about? No doubt your next plan to abolish the few nerves I have left. You'll be the death of me, Hester—you're going to kill me one of these days!"

"I'm not lethal, Ma," I said.

"Don't you realize you're ruining the family name every time that you do something like this?"

"The name will be fine too—I have a different one now, remember? It came with the marriage license."

She was at a dead end. I was almost gone—maybe just a few more sentences—and there was nothing she could do.

"Hester! Now listen to me, I want you to find out where you are. There must be some road sign. Find out where you are—ask the cashier!"

"Sure I can ask the cashier, but that's not why I called."

"Then I guess I'll just have this call traced."

I shrugged my shoulders. "Well, that's up to you, but most likely we won't be here anymore. And even if we ever ran into each other again? Then what? What do you think you could possibly do? I didn't kidnap anyone this time."

She said nothing, and I decided I might as well continue. "It's nothing personal, Mom. It's really not. We're just not from the same planet, and we shouldn't pretend we are. Genetics threw us together, but that doesn't mean we have to *agree* on things. There's no use in righteous finger-pointing, don't you see that? Because it all comes down to the fact that we're helpless against anyone else's ideals."

I could tell by the unusual breathing pattern coming from the receiver that she wasn't quite as gung-ho as I was about this theory.

"Are you with that disgusting man—O'Brien or whatever his name is? You are, aren't you?"

"Flaherty. Yeah, I'm with him."

"I knew it! Don't you realize you're letting this man ruin your life?"

I laughed. "Oddly enough, that is the one thought I've never had regarding him. I've had just about every other thought."

"Well, you never were the smart one. But I'm warning you, you'll regret every minute of your life."

"I won't regret it. It's a nasty habit."

There was a pause.

"Don't you ever come back here, Hester. Don't you ever come home and tell me to sort it all out. Those days are over, you hear me?"

"I know they are."

Again a pause. This one drew out longer than the others. I shifted my weight to my right foot and decided to say what I'd called for, and I was halfway through the word "good-bye" when she hung up.

Jethro and I sat opposite each other in the school playground. It was three in the afternoon, school was just out, and there was a lot of screaming and running around. He was wearing the "Metal Up Your Ass" T-shirt that we'd bought him in Arkansas to balance out that Christmas wardrobe a little, and his black hair was softly wafting in the wind. His backpack lay at his feet and his fingers were stretched around an astrology book that I had brought him from the library. We were in Miami. The heat was coming at us with the waves of the breeze, and we just sat there on the bench, smiling at each other. We had so much to say that nothing was coming out. Our acquaintance had ended abruptly at the Kansas City airport. We didn't have a chance to say anything at all that day. In fact, I don't think we said anything at all. We might have exchanged heavy glances. I can't remember. Anyway, what *should* we have said? "Well, honey, I guess shit happens. Maybe I'll see you again when you've got a beer belly and a beard"? I mean, what could we possibly have said that would have *mattered*? We understood in the true melodramatic sense that it was better just to walk away and become friends with eternity.

Well, eternity didn't turn out to be half as long as expected, 'cause now there we sat, in front of an elementary school. Sunlight, spring breeze, children's laughter, and everything else that belongs in commercials for fabric softener.

"What's it feel like, being a child safely retrieved from a kidnapping?" I asked.

"Good."

It's always nice to know that you haven't ruined a child's life.

"I'm part of the robotics club now," he went on. "We're entering this competition. Schools all over the country are making these robots, and they're going to compete with each other in April. Our whole class is going to go to Washington, D.C. They're renting a bus for that. But one of those real buses, you know, that have a toilet in the back and TVs and everything."

"Oh yeah, those are great."

"And I have a girlfriend now too. Her name's Dolores. She's Mexican."

"No shit! How the hell did *that* happen?"

He shrugged his shoulders. "I was just standing by the water fountain. And she came up and told me she was psychic. So I told her about Jesus Freak. And then I told her about Lorna and Elvin being aliens, and how we had to leave in the middle of the night and about the cop and how we were in jail and we had to escape through the air-conditioning—"

"What air-conditioning? We never went to jail."

His smile became wide and bottomless. "Well, I couldn't tell her that we just sat around drinking hot chocolate all day at the police station!"

He had a point.

"I guess you're right about that. So, what happened?"

"We fell in love."

I raised my eyebrows. "You fell in *love* while talking about Jesus Freak over the water fountain? Just like that?"

"Mm-hmm. We're probably going to get married when we're grown up."

I won't lie. I was surprised.

"Jesus. I really didn't expect you to be an engaged man before your eleventh birthday."

"Don't worry. We're not doing anything—you know—from page thirteen of that book."

"Glad to hear it."

He nodded. "We're not going to start doing *that* kind of stuff until we get into eleventh grade."

"You've got it all planned out, huh?"

"Yeah."

"Well, listen, when you get into eleventh grade you and I are going to have a little talk, okay? Your mom's a nice lady, but there are certain subject matters I just don't trust her with."

"Okay."

"And just so you know, I'm very jealous, Jethro."

That pleased him in a vague way.

"You're going to be one hell of a lover someday. And you know why?"

"Why?"

"Because you have a way with words. You tell girls what they want to hear, and you actually mean it. Even if it didn't happen—like in the case of the escape from jail through the air-conditioning."

He beamed. The only visual of physical love he probably possessed was of two frogs mating in the pages of a library book. But his instincts told him that the compliment I had just given him reached far down into the depths of what makes a man. His cheeks burned bright red, and his words seemed momentarily lost among the thick subtropical grass at our feet. I keep forgetting he was only ten.

"Well, I guess I'm going to have to get used to the fact that you'll be married to another woman."

"Well, you're married to Fenton!"

"You thought I forgot that?"

We both glanced across the street where Arlene stood parked in the sunlight in all her glory. Fenton was standing beside her, elaborately trying to explain to a bunch of six-year-olds why they shouldn't throw tennis balls against his camper. The kids started laughing and one of them, a little boy with heavy glasses and a mischievous face of contentment, continued to bounce his ball off the side of the camper. Fenton began threatening him. Each threat brought on a new wave of laughter from the crowd that went up to his waist.

"What about you?" Jethro asked, all of a sudden losing his

bashfulness and looking up with torpedo eyes. He had that way of growing old within a matter of seconds. "Did they ever decapitate you in the backyard?"

"Nope. I almost decapitated *myself*, though."

"You did?"

"Yeah, I discovered that if you drink enough vodka or rubbing alcohol, you'll feel much more miserable."

"Really?"

"Yeah."

"What about your mom?"

"What about her?"

"Why'd she let you go this time?"

"Well, it turns out that it's not up to her where I go."

He rolled his eyes with disbelief. "I told you that like three million times."

"Yeah, I know. I know you did, but you're much faster that way. I personally never understand things until they get real bad," I said, smiling. "And unfortunately I probably wouldn't like it any other way."

He understood that for some reason.

"And you know what else?" I continued. "My mom is okay. In a weird way, of course—she's definitely not okay in a normal way, but in her own twisted way, she's all right."

"I thought you said she was a dangerous lunatic."

"I'm not saying that she's *not*," I said. "I'm only saying that she's got dreams, like anyone else. Her dreams happen to be a life like a five o'clock in the afternoon soap opera. You ever watched one of those?"

"No."

"Well, good, because there's more interesting things to be

doing with your time—like folding laundry. Someone's always ly-ing in some hospital bed giving long monologues over bad music. You know, that kind of stuff—bad actors staring each other down, lots of crying, screaming, and holding on to some ex-husband's ankles as he tries to storm out to be with your best friend."

Jethro seemed impressed.

"Anyway, I'm making it sound better than it actually is. Point is, my mom would just shit in her pants from ecstasy if her life could be like that. It's a valid dream; I just don't fit into it. It's really hard on her that I don't do drugs. I don't even have weight issues or cut myself or anything. I mean, I did kidnap you and she got a lot out of that, but it didn't last long enough. It's obviously not going to work out, no matter how hard we try. I don't fit the bill. It's that simple."

There was a short silence. Fenton's argument with the six-year-olds came drifting to us from across the street.

"The point is," I said, "it's not her fault that she's a pain in my ass."

"So you left."

"Yeah, but this time I didn't kidnap my cousin." I shrugged my shoulders. "You live and learn."

You really do. I figure you can't live and *not* learn. Back in the camper I taped the napkin with Jethro's phone number onto the kitchen cabinet next to the plastic wristwatch. Then I crawled up front and we pulled out of the six-year-old mob with their tennis balls. A couple of the balls went bouncing off the back one last time.

MAYBE IT WAS strange at first, being in the camper without Jesus Freak or Jethro. Seeing landscapes through the windows that weren't part of winter anymore. Knowing that we weren't running from something or meeting a destination. Feeling old. Ancient even. How can you not feel superior to life after having been a nationally televised kidnapper? How can you not feel weathered after spending many nauseous afternoons daydreaming by the edge of shit creek? Ever know that wanting someone who's not there can make food taste bad? It's the darndest thing—I figured that one out when I hadn't eaten in three days and the thought of having a perfectly decent meal made my stomach turn. I couldn't help but realize that ecstasy is nothing more than peace of mind. Sometimes you just feel at home with an asshole. I don't think I cared to worry about what kind of home that would be—whether we'd ever kiss again or whether we were just siblings now. But it was good to know that when I smiled at him, he would smile right back, because although he knows he's breaking all the asshole rules, he can't help it, and he'd break a million noses just to find me again in that hospital elevator.

I stared at Fenton.

"*What?*" he asked.

"Nothing."

ACKNOWLEDGMENTS

I WOULD LIKE to thank the following people for getting their hands dirty and directly contributing to the existence of this book: Grainne Fox, William Clark, Kerri Kolen, Ed Victor, Madeleine Webber, Renate Helnwein, and Gottfried Helnwein.

My family: Ali, Cyril, Amadeus, Jenni, and Croí Helnwein.

Those people who have thrown help in my way while I was writing this and made sure I stumbled over it and somehow came out the other end with the story in its final form: Chris Watson, Vivian Gray, Natasha Gray, Alex Prager, Hans Janitschek, Peter Plate, Jason Lee, Justin Shady, Dave Crosland, Lolo Dahl, Bryten Goss, Tiffany Steffens, Kevin Llewellyn, Mella Ottensteiner, Virginia MacGregor, Danny Masterson, WESC, Josie Hamilton, and Rachel Rose Desimone.

My eternal and bottomless gratitude also to Tom Waits, The White Stripes, Bob Dylan, Blind Willie McTell, Robert Johnson, Charlie Patton, Mark Twain, John Steinbeck, and Fernando Pessoa. I owe them all a love letter.

Thank you to all my friends and everyone who thought it was neat when I said I was writing a book.

ABOUT THE AUTHOR

BORN IN VIENNA, AUSTRIA, Mercedes Helnwein began writing and drawing at an early age, developing a deep fascination for both fields. In 2000, she began to divide her time between Los Angeles and Ireland, exhibiting her art and writing short stories and essays for literary journals. With influences ranging from the Southern Gothic tradition to the cartoons of Robert Crumb, nineteenth-century Russian literature, American motel culture, and the Delta blues, Helnwein's work began to take on a style of its own, and resulted, among other things, in her first novel, *The Potential Hazards of Hester Day*. She is currently living in Ireland and Los Angeles, exhibiting her art internationally, and working on her second novel.